Yep, my bro's a veg.

It's funny, though, that in some ways I sometimes kind of envy Shawn. He doesn't have a clue in the world about what's happening around him. He just sits there and drools and goes "ahhhhh" all day. He doesn't worry about the stuff that makes my life crazy, like what college might take him or whether he's going to get an athletic scholarship, or anything at all. My life, a lot of the time, feels like a car roaring down the freeway in cruise control, where you don't even have to touch the gas, only I'm on bald tires going 120 miles per hour, wild-ass flying, and I have no idea where I'm headed, and maybe the cruise control is broken and I can't even slow down. Shawn never worries about that kind of crap. He can't worry about anything, since he's got no brain.

ALSO BY TERRY TRUEMAN

Inside Out

Stuck in Neutral
A Michael L. Printz Honor Book

TERRY TRUEMAN

CRUISE CONTROL

HARPERTEMPEST
AN IMPRINT OF HARPERCOLLINS*PUBLISHERS*

Cruise Control
Copyright © 2004 by Terry Trueman

Library of Congress Cataloging-in-Publication Data
Trueman, Terry.
    Cruise control / Terry Trueman.— 1st ed.
      p.   cm.
    Companion to: Stuck in neutral.
    Summary: A talented basketball player struggles to deal with the
helplessness and anger that come with having a brother rendered
completely dysfunctional by severe cerebral palsy and a father who
deserted the family.
    ISBN-10: 0-06-447377-5 (pbk.)
    ISBN-13: 978-0-06-447377-4 (pbk.)
    [1. Brothers—Fiction. 2. Cerebral palsy—Fiction. 3. People with
disabilities—Fiction. 4. Anger—Fiction. 5. Fathers and sons—
Fiction. 6. Basketball—Fiction.] I. Title.
PZ7.T7813Cr 2004   2003019822
[Fic]—dc22   CIP
                                                            AC

Typography by Andrea Vandergrift
13 14 15 LP/RRDH 20 19 18 17 16 15 14 13 12 11
❖
First paperback edition, 2005
Visit us on the World Wide Web!
www.harpertempest.com

For Antonia Markiet

ACKNOWLEDGMENTS

This is a tough book for which to offer acknowledgments in that it came so quickly. I wanted to write a sequel to *Stuck in Neutral*, but a sequel would have "ruined the ending," as my editor Toni Markiet pointed out; we were walking back from lunch in New York City when Toni suggested, "Why not write a companion novel to *Stuck in Neutral*, something from some other character's point of view?" I liked the idea immediately, and thus *Cruise Control* started to become a reality.

I have already dedicated this book to Toni, so now I have to thank all the usual suspects: My family: wife, Patti; sons, Jesse and Sheehan; all the Eggers; my dad and his wife; and sister Cindy and Garren. At HarperCollins, Meghan Dietsche, Phoebe Yeh, Colleen Schwartz, cover design artist Cliff Nielsen, and everyone else involved in making this book. At Sterling Lord Literistic Inc., the "great man": George Nicholson, my agent, and his intrepid partner in crime, Paul "it's-okay-to-call-me-Pauly" Rodeen, and my movie guy Jody Hotchkiss (formerly with SLL, Inc.). Colleagues who have helped are led by Kelly Milner-Halls, Chris Crutcher, Terry Davis, Michael Gurian, Eddie-Jim Averett, and Mary.

Thanks to everyone who has been involved in the creation of *Cruise Control*. Thanks to the many critics whose appreciation and thoughtful consideration of my earlier books make this book possible. All the librarians and English teachers who have sponsored/suffered my visits and presentations and kept me from almost certain jail terms by their friendships and protectiveness. All of ALA, most especially YALSA. Most importantly, of course, thank you to all my readers, so many of whom have taken the time to tell me how excited they are to see this book and without whose encouragement and support, again, there would probably be no book. To any of you who have written me and not received a response, please forgive me. Who else? Sorry, I'm drawing a blank—but you know who you are and you know how bad I'll feel that I've left you off this list.

"*. . . the possibility of the miracle is here with us*
almost every day . . ."
—*Charles Bukowski, "60 Yard Pass"*
From War All the Time:
Poems 1981–1984

CRUISE
CONTROL

CHAPTER ONE

My only brother is a veg. Yep, a full-fledged, drooling, fourteen-year-old idiot. If you were to call him that, you'd have a big problem on your hands—namely, *me*! But in fact, that's what my bro is. His name is Shawn, and he's got a totally whacked-out brain.

My name is Paul, but don't call me Pauly. I mean *never*. Two things annoy me more than anything else. First, anybody being mean to my brother, second, being called Pauly.

Shawn lives with us—my sister, Cindy, and my mom, Lindy, and me—in our house here on Queen Anne Hill in Seattle. My dad, a piece of butt fluff named Sydney McDaniel, moved out on the rest of us a long time ago. After he left, he wrote a poem about my brother, won a dumb-ass Pulitzer Prize, got all famous, and now thinks he's cool. My dad wouldn't stay with us and help us take care of my brother—no, he left me to handle all that so he could jet around and make a bunch of money whining about his tragic plight. He makes me want to puke. In case this isn't clear yet—I pretty much *hate* my dad.

Yeah, I've got what you might call a bad temper. Officially, I suppose you could say it's an "anger management" problem, although I've never had to go talk to a school counselor or anybody about it. Hey, it's not as big a problem for me as for the guys whose butts I kick. And every time I lose my temper and worry that I'm going too far, all I have to do is think about my old man, and *bam*, it's like hitting my violence refresh key.

My brother, Shawn, the veg, is sitting across the room from me right now. He's in his wheelchair, sitting where Mom always sets him, in front of the window looking out at the Olympic Mountains and Puget Sound. There's this big strand of spit hanging off Shawn's lower lip down onto the front of his T-shirt and coveralls. Shawn's T-shirt is a Denver

Broncos–Orange Crush number, about twenty years old. I think it used to belong to my dad. Dad left lots of his useless junk here when he moved out.

Shawn's also wearing special coveralls because he wears diapers and these coveralls have tear-apart inseams—you know, like the Velcro tear-apart warm-ups they give you for sports. Why Mom doesn't use regular warm-up pants, so that Shawn doesn't look like such a totally messed-up dweeb, is a mystery to me. I even gave Mom two pair of my old warm-ups that I had left over after my sophomore and junior varsity b-ball seasons. No good. Mom's committed to making sure Shawn looks moronic, and he does.

Now Shawn is going "ahhhhhh . . . ahhhhhh" over and over again, just making noise to entertain himself. He does this a lot; it's actually pretty irritating. Shawn is "profoundly developmentally disabled." That's what the doctors call him. He can't feed himself, walk, talk, or do anything at all. Yep, my bro's a veg.

It's funny, though, that in some ways I sometimes kind of envy Shawn. He doesn't have a clue in the world about what's happening around him. He just sits there and drools and goes "ahhhh" all day.

He doesn't worry about the stuff that makes my life crazy, like what college might take him or whether he's going to get an athletic scholarship, or anything at all. My life, a lot of the time, feels like a car roaring down the freeway in cruise control, where you don't even have to touch the gas, only I'm on bald tires going 120 miles per hour, wild-ass flying, and I have no idea where I'm headed, and maybe the cruise control is broken and I can't even slow down. Shawn never worries about that kind of crap. He can't worry about anything, since he's got no brain.

Suddenly there's a huge gasping sound and I know that it's not quite true that Shawn has *no* brain. You can't have a seizure, like he's having right now, if you don't have any brain at all. I walk over to Shawn. His seizure, something they call a grand mal, starts with a crazy-sounding laugh and a strange, completely weird smile. But now his face is twisted and quivering, lips a bluish-purple color, eyes staring and glazed over. His arms, hands, and legs shake and vibrate as the electrical crap in his brain slams his body. There's a sickening odor coming from him, like the smell of vomit. As I reach his side, I hear him choking and gagging.

I touch his head gently, letting my hand rest

above his ear, and now I brush his hair back off his forehead like I've seen Mom do a thousand times when she's helping him through a seizure. Saliva pours out of his mouth, and for almost a whole minute, since that first gasping sound, he can't breathe. His face turns redder and redder until finally he gasps loud again and collapses into his chair. He starts to breathe normally and his color turns a yellowish pale. Every time this seizure crap happens, I worry about what if he doesn't start breathing again.

So Shawn's got a brain all right—a *useless* one that does nothing but hurt him.

"I sometimes kind of envy Shawn"? Right—what the hell was I thinking, especially since *I'm* the guy most other kids envy?

At the risk of sounding full of myself (hey, it's not bragging if you can back it up), I'm the best athlete in our school. I was last year too, even though I was only in eleventh grade then. I've been the starting quarterback on our football team since halfway through our sophomore year. I'm starting point guard and captain on our basketball team, and I play third base, the hot corner, on our baseball team. If you asked any kid in our school who is the studliest jock, they'd tell you it's me. I also get straight As. Sorry, but it's all true.

How sick is this: I'm the major jock-stud in a high school of over eighteen hundred kids, but my brother has the brain of a badminton birdie and a body to match. I've got everything and he's got nothing. I'm a three-year, three-sport letterman and Shawn can't even stand up! Like I said, sick, huh?

Sometimes life really sucks!

CHAPTER TWO

Like I said, I've got a temper. It's so bad, it makes me sick sometimes. Last summer these two bullies were picking on Shawn, and I almost burned them alive. Really, I flipped out and poured gasoline all over them and then tried to set them on fire. Only my sister, Cindy, stopped me from doing it. Hey, they were picking on little messed-up, in-a-wheelchair, idiot Shawn—these two wads were flicking a Bic lighter right under Shawn's chin and laughing at him! But worse than my nearly killing them—something else happened that day that I don't talk about. Maybe that's why I'm so pissed off all the time, but I don't know for sure and I don't even like to *think* about it, so never mind.

But being the brother to a kid like Shawn isn't easy. I love him because he's my brother, but he can't do or feel anything, I mean *anything*, and it's hard to love someone who can't love back. Then, of course, you feel like a total butt wad to say something like that because it basically means that the only reason you love somebody is to get their love in return, which is pretty selfish. There's probably some big psychological explanation to why fighting, even though I hate it, sometimes feels so good to me and why I often think about Shawn and my dad and our family being so messed up when I'm kicking the crap out of somebody—but to be honest, I don't really care about psychology. All I know is that sometimes I feel like I'm going to explode, and fighting, as sick as it feels afterward, gives me some kind of weird relief.

My baddest fights actually happen in my dreams. In these dreams, a lot of the times it's my dad and me going at it, and he's tough and tall and stronger than he is in real life, and he's hurting me. Shawn is usually there, sitting back in his wheelchair, real quiet, just watching us. But finally I always get the upper hand on my old man, and as I'm pounding on him, he wants me to quit. But no matter how much he begs, no matter how hurt he is, I can't seem to stop. These dreams are nightmares really; sometimes I've got blood all over my hands and Dad's face is being shredded. It's always ugly and messy and horrible.

Why do I hate my dad so much? Isn't it obvious? He left us. He ran away from Mom and Cindy and me, but most of all from Shawn. How could Dad abandon a kid who needs him like Shawn does? And how can I ever go anywhere or do anything with my life when I'm the only guy left around here? How can I go away to college and leave Mom and Shawn with nobody to watch out for them? My dad is a self-centered jerk. If he didn't send money every month to pay for our family's expenses, I'd give him the bloody, vicious ass whippin' he deserves for ruining my life and for running out on my brother. Since I'm not allowed kick my dad's ass, I guess maybe sometimes I take it out on other people.

But I worry that someday, fighting the way I do, I'm going to go too far and get into serious trouble. So I try to push all this out of my mind and concentrate on sports—where I always work harder than anybody else. Right now, it's basketball season. I love hoops, and it helps me keep from being crazy.

What else can I do?

CHAPTER THREE

It's Tuesday afternoon at basketball practice. The way Coach Davis does practice is that when we first come out, he has us all grab the rock and start shooting from various spots on the court. After a few minutes of this shoot-around, once we're a little warmed up, Coach blows his whistle and everybody stops. Whoever's holding a ball gets one more shot, and if you make it, the ball is rebounded and tossed back to you, then you take a couple steps back, or to the side, and after somebody else takes a turn, you shoot again. This keeps happening, everybody taking turns back and forth, until you miss. Once you do, you take a slow warm-up jog around the outside of the court. Shoot-around keeps going until everyone has missed and we're all jogging together. Obviously, the better a shooter you are, the less you have to run. Shoot-around usually lasts for about ten minutes; I like it 'cause I'm a shooter.

Coach blows his whistle. I have a ball in my hands and Coach yells to me.

"McDaniel, you're up."

I'm about ten feet out, a little to the right side, and I put up a nice, arching jump shot. *Swish*.

Coach yells to Hank Kliment. "The Hankster," our huge center, is only about six feet away from the backboard, right in front; he puts up one of his classic, beeline brick jumpers that, of course, clanks off the rim. The Hankster is *not* a shooter. Everybody laughs and Hank moans.

"Have nice run, 'ster," somebody yells. Hank gives us all a death-ray stare that makes everybody laugh even more.

"McDaniel," Coach calls again. I take a couple steps back and I shoot. The ball ticks the rim just a hair but goes through real easy.

Coach yells to John-Boy Reich.

Reich shoots, makes it, and we keep going around.

Because I don't miss, I move farther and farther away from the basket with each shot, way off to the left, way off to the right, way behind the key. But the weirdest thing happens. It's like I *can't* miss. I mean, I'm not trying to miss, of course, but most times I would have missed by now. My teammate and best friend, Tim "Tim-bo" Gunther, hangs in with me for a while, hitting six or seven shots before he misses, but after a couple dozen shots, I'm the only guy left shooting. The rest of the guys stop running and watch me. I hit another half dozen shots, and everybody starts to cheer.

All kinds of strange crap starts going through my head: I think about if I miss, it will mean my dad's a way cool guy—*swoosh*. I think about if I make it, it'll mean I'm gonna get a full-ride scholarship to Georgetown and be the greatest point guard since Allen Iverson—*swish*. I even think about if I hit this shot, it means that my veg brother will someday learn to talk and walk and be all right— nothing but net. The weirdest thought, though, is impossible to explain—it's not even a thought, it's a feeling. What I mean is that it is for moments like this that I love playing sports: Right this second I'm not thinking about Shawn or my dad or anybody or anything; right now, the truth is, it feels like my feet are barely even touching the ground, I'm floating, soaring on the pure energy of this shooting touch. It's like nothing can hurt me. It feels like I could almost fly. . . .

Coach interrupts the magic by yelling to me, "One more, hot dog, from the opposite foul line. You make this and we cancel ball breakers at the end of practice."

"Ball breakers" are wind sprints, which everyone hates; Coach makes us run them for conditioning. By "opposite foul line," Coach means that he wants me to shoot a ridiculous seventy-footer, almost the full length of the court.

I answer Coach, "If I hit it, we cancel ball breakers for the rest of the week." As team captain, I can jerk his chain a little.

"It's a deal," Coach says, "but you gotta shoot with your eyes closed."

A groan goes up from the sidelines, but I give them my oh-ye-of-little-faith look, and everybody shuts up.

I answer, "You got it."

Coach never has us shoot stupid shots like this;

he always has us focus on shots that might save a win for us, shots that could actually happen in a game situation. But I hustle down to the opposite foul line and take a couple steps back so that I can really step into the throw.

I study the distance a little and bounce the ball a couple times. Everybody is quiet. I hear the Hankster and some of the other big guys who *really* hate ball breakers mumbling prayers, which makes me smile. I look at the basket seventy feet away, get a good read on the distance, then close my eyes; I bounce the ball, take my steps, and loft the shot.

I keep my head down; I don't even watch the ball go but just keep my eyes shut, thinking about all the shots I've made and about how perfect my touch has been, about flying, soaring, and about how freaky—

The cheers just about blow me over. You'd think we just won Districts.

All the guys rush me and start pounding on me.

Coach smiles and says, "I think you snuck a peek, but I can't prove it. Okay, slackers, a couple more laps to break another sweat, and if hot-hand doesn't mind, I think we'll get on with a little actual *basketball* practice."

As we all start to run, the Hankster jogs up behind me and says softly, "You got us out of ball breakers for a week. . . . I wanna have your child!"

Normally this kind of challenge to my heterosexual pride would not be allowed. The Hankster is 6 feet, 9 inches and weighs 286, which wouldn't dissuade me a bit. But we need the 'ster's bulk in the middle if we're gonna win this season, so I'll let him live.

John-Boy Reich comes up behind me and says, "That was pretty amazing, bro."

I snap back at him, "I'm not your bro."

I've got a brother, and John-Boy ain't him. Suddenly somebody shoves me from behind and I look around fast, but it's Tim Gunther smiling at me. Tim-bo says, "Lighten up, man—John-Boy didn't mean anything bad."

I take a couple deep breaths, and I smile back at Tim. I know he's right. It's just that word, "bro," the way people throw it around so off-the-cuff. I hate that. It always reminds me about the incredible unfairness of the world, and about what a sadistic madman God must be to have thrown Shawn and me into the same family—when I think of that crap, all I feel is bummed.

John-Boy walks away without another word. I'm such a dumb-ass! "Hey," I yell to him. "You owe me for ball breakers and don't forget it!"

He smiles back at me. It's okay. This time.

CHAPTER FOUR

After practice I walk out of the gym and head for my car. I've got an older Honda. It's not a junker, but it's not exactly a luxury ride either. I've got a stereo system that hits pretty hard, though, so rides home are always one of my favorite times to chill.

Eddie Farr yells over to me, "Hey, Paul, can I catch a lift?"

I answer, "Sure."

So much for chillin'. The idea of spending any time with Eddie Farr isn't all that appealing, but what are you gonna do?

You know how some guys are just so dumb that they can't seem to help saying moronic things without meaning any harm? Why is it that guys like this are always weak and defenseless, too?

"How's your sister?" Eddie asks.

This is exactly what I mean!

I know that Eddie would cut off the little fingers of both hands to get into my sister's pants. He *has* to know that I know this. Does he really think that I'm going to pimp for him?

I tell Eddie, "She's in a Turkish prison."

He looks confused; then he changes the subject, saying, "I saw your dad on TV."

"Oh yeah?" I answer. "Was that on *America's Ten Biggest Assholes*?"

"I don't think so," Eddie answers. "We don't have cable."

He's serious about the cable thing.

I say, "Actually, Eddie, I think that's a *Fox* program."

"Really?" Eddie asks. He's sincere. He wants to know if Fox really has a program called *America's Ten Biggest Assholes*. Unbelievable.

So it goes: Eddie keeps asking dumb questions and making bizarre conversation, hitting on stuff for which, if I were drunk or didn't know how pitiful he is, I'd beat him half to death—and I keep flipping him smart-ass answers.

But there's this thing about Eddie that forces me to deal with him: I hate to admit this, and I know that when I do it makes me look like the selfish, total jerk that I am, but the truth is that Eddie's always treated Shawn *better* than I do. What I mean is that ever since we were little kids, Eddie's never seemed to understand that Shawn doesn't know anything, and that Shawn doesn't have a clue about what's going on. I went to elementary school and middle school and now I go to high school with Eddie Farr. I've known him since we were in second grade. He's one of those guys who love to run the VCR and who actually *enjoy* pop quizzes. He's never had a girlfriend or even a date. But Eddie's known Shawn all our lives; he used to come to Shawn's birthday parties, back when Mom was still into throwing a birthday party for Shawn even though my bro didn't have the slightest idea what was going on.

And Eddie's always talked to Shawn and told him jokes, kidded with him, never teasing or being mean, just treating Shawn like he was normal or something. Not very many kids are that way with Shawn. I know *I'm* not, and I feel guilty about it. So

Eddie, for all his freakish, subnormal weirdness is cool. I kid with him and I don't ever treat him bad, like the total social disaster that he is. Eddie couldn't care less about popularity or fitting in, but whether he knows it or not, he's built up a lifetime of protection and credit with me. This doesn't mean I like him or hang out with him. It just means what it means, which includes giving him this ride home.

Finally we get to his house, only a few blocks from my place.

"Bye-bye, Paul," Eddie says as he gets out of the car; not "Later" or "Peace" or "I'm out" or anything remotely normal, just "Bye-bye."

He leans back in the window and asks, "How's Shawn?"

"He's doin' real good," I say. "He's been working on cures for AIDS and leukemia."

Eddie looks confused. Then he smiles a slightly funny smile and says, "Oh, good one."

If Eddie weren't Eddie, if I didn't know how much he actually *likes* Shawn, I'd be tempted to jump out of the car and hit him a few times on the chance that his funny grin is a smirk, but I know it's not.

Eddie's last words are "Thanks for the lift, and say hi to your sister for me."

"Right," I say. I almost go back to the thing about the Turkish prison, because I *really* like that one, but that'd be like casting pearls into a hopeless Eddie fog, so I let it slide.

I hit the gas instead.

Spending time with Eddie Farr is somehow strangely relaxing. I don't know, maybe it's that Eddie is so simple and easy to read. Maybe it's the way Eddie asked about Shawn, like he was a normal guy or something. Whatever it is, I feel good.

I can't imagine anything that could wreck my mood right now.

CHAPTER FIVE

When I pull up to our house, my dad's car is here. Damn!

I consider rolling right on by, killing time until he leaves, since he never stays very long when Shawn's home from school. But the hell with it, this is *my* house, not his. He's the one who moved away, so screw him.

I pull up to my regular parking spot and cut the engine.

When I walk through the front door, I see that Mom and Dad are out on the deck. Shawn's with them, in his wheelchair, "ahhhhhhing." Way to go, Shawn, bet the old man *loves* that.

I stop for just a second and stare at the three of them—what an odd crew: Dad's been coming around more lately, which sucks; much as I hate him for abandoning Shawn, it's even worse to have him keep bouncing in and out—if he wants to be here, why doesn't he stay, if he wants to leave, why doesn't he just go! Shawn's always the same, except that his seizures seem to have been getting a little worse; Mom's a rock and always has been, capable of putting up with Dad's total selfishness in ways that I can't. I quietly set my backpack on the chair by the front door and make a quick move through the living room and up the stairway.

"Hey, Pauly . . ." Dad calls after me.

I pretend not to hear him, taking the stairs two at a time. As soon as I'm in my room, I strip outa my warm-ups, grab my robe, and head to the shower. With any luck at all, Dad will already be gone when I come out. That'll be fine by me. No phoniness, no "How you doin?" "Not bad, how's yerself?" I hate that. I can't stand him and I don't give a rat's ass what he thinks of me.

As I'm showering, I think back to the freaky thing, my shooting streak that happened at shoot-around during practice today. It was so weird. After we all jogged together awhile, I came back down to earth—there's not much soaring going on when you're running in circles with a bunch of sweaty teammates. We started to scrimmage. I missed my first three shots and a couple guys laughed, which bugged me and made me work even harder. I smacked the laughers around a little, well-placed elbows, outhustling them for boards, stuff like that. As team captain, I can get away with a little nastiness. Pretty soon my shots started falling again, but by then nobody was laughing anymore anyway.

I wonder if anybody else at our school ever had a shooting run at shoot-around like the one I had today? I wonder if—

"Hey, buddy!"

Damnit! It's my dad. I forgot to lock the door.

I snap back at him, "Do you mind!"

He hesitates and says, "Sorry . . . I just wanted to say good-bye. I'm taking off. I wanted to—"

"Later," I say, interrupting him. I think, Good riddance, but resist saying it out loud.

"You doin' all right?" he asks.

"Yeah, great," I say. Then I quickly add, "At least I *will* be once you close that door and stop letting all the warm air out of here."

"Sure . . . sorry," Dad says, ignoring my smart-ass tone.

Suddenly Dad's cell phone, hanging on this little hook jobby on his belt, rings its dumb-ass chiming-music ring. He should have this phone surgically implanted onto the side of his head, he uses it so much. As he grabs his phone, he says to me, "Okay, I'll see you later."

"Yeah," I answer, thinking, Not if I see you first.

Dad starts yakking on his cell before he even closes the door.

I put my head back into the shower, turn the hot up, and feel it steaming, almost scalding my neck and scalp—it's like I want to burn him off me. It's like talking to him is so gross that I'd be willing to dive into boiling water to miss it.

I just can't stand the phoniness: "Good-bye, Pauly-boy," "Good-bye, Da-da."

God, I hate him.

CHAPTER SIX

I'm at school, sitting in second period, my Current World Problems class, when who should come waltzing past the window but my favorite jerk wad in the world—Daddy! Wonderful.

Mom warned me this might happen. And now I'm sitting in a classroom where there's this clear view of the main entrance to the school and Papa Butt Munch is making his typical *grand entry* right where I have to look at him. Of course, as he walks, he's talking on his cell phone—what an idiot.

Some of the kids in class glance out and see him too. Because of his Pulitzer Prize, Dad's on TV pretty often, so a lot of people recognize him. Right now he also happens to have some guy carrying a big metal suitcase in one hand and a huge TV camera in the other trailing along right behind him. Way to go, Dad—now everyone is sure to realize what a truly big, *big*, BIG-time celebrity you are—a legend in your own mind.

A soft murmur starts swirling around the room. I keep my eyes glued to the copy of *Time* magazine that Mr. Jenkins gave us. About half the class watches this ridiculous Sydney-McDaniel-Famous-Prima-Donna routine. Even Mr. Jenkins is looking.

I swear to God, if anybody mentions that he's my dad, I'll nail 'em.

"Hey, Paul, there's your father."

Eddie Farr. Perfect.

Of course now *everybody* in class looks at me and then out the window.

Maybe I *can* beat Eddie up—maybe just this one time I can kick the living crap out of him. . . .

"Looks like he's going to be on TV again," Eddie observes.

"You think?" I ask sarcastically

"Well, he's got that cameraman guy with him and—"

"Eddie, shut the hell up," I say in a low voice.

Nobody sitting close to us goes "uuuuuu" or "ohhhhhh" or makes any joking sounds; a lot of kids in school have seen my temper before.

Eddie quickly says, "Sorry."

I remember now what Mom said, something about Dad doing some kind of PBS thing, "sometime this week." I think it's about Shawn and kids with handicaps. I don't know, really. I didn't listen much after she said, "Your dad might be dropping by your school." But it doesn't surprise me that the old man is trying to figure yet another angle about how to make himself famous off my brother— that's the meat and potatoes of Dad's career, being a tragic, famous retard-dad. For him to come to our school, though, might be a new low.

The whole school thing is pretty weird for me, anyway. I've never liked school, all the rules and childishness, but I've always been good at my classes and loved playing sports. I skipped fourth grade, and by taking summer school classes, I'm finishing high school early. I'll be done this January instead of in June, when my sister, Cindy, gets done. I'll qualify for jock scholarships before any of my competition. Of course, all of this assumes that I could actually go away to college; my old man pretty much ruined that when he ran out on us.

Speaking of Dickhead Dad, he and the camera-man just went into the administration building and are finally out of sight, thank God. Mr. Jenkins glances over at me, and it actually looks like he's going to say something about Dad. I quickly look away from him. He doesn't say anything after all.

I don't know if Mr. Jenkins has ever read Dad's writing about Shawn or not. I don't know if Mr. Jenkins even knows I have a brother here at school. Luckily, it's a huge school, so I see Shawn only once in a while. Sometimes I catch a glimpse of him as he's being rolled along in his wheelchair down the hall. Seeing him drooling and so out of it always kills me. Also, the special-ed kids deliver coffee to the teachers first period, and once in a while, Shawn is hauled along on these trips with some of his retarded classmates and a teacher's aide.

I've been sitting in class when this crew comes in, and it's totally weird. Some kids know that Shawn and I are related—kids like Eddie Farr, who've known us for a long time. But whenever I see Shawn, like by instinct, I always look around to see who's staring at him . . . staring at *me*!

Shawn will be in his wheelchair drooling and going "ahhhhhh." And some kids will glance at me, and then look away real fast. Some of the other kids, ones who don't know Shawn and I are brothers, might stare at him, nudging each other and laughing at the retard. I always feel pissed at those kids, and sometimes, later, away from school so I won't get in trouble, I'll kick their asses.

But one thing I *never* do is to acknowledge Shawn in any way, and I feel like the weakest, most cowardly wimp in the world for that. In my heart, I want to go over and pat his head and say something to him; I want to stand with him and hug him and let the whole world know he's my brother, but I can't ever bring myself to do it. I just can't. I don't have the guts any more than my old man does. Which makes us *both* chickens. Like father, like son, right?

CHAPTER SEVEN

The rest of the day of Dad's visit to the school passes without my seeing him again. Sometimes you just catch a break.

I'm back home now, shooting hoops with Tim-bo, who's the best player on our basketball team next to me. He's also a guard, and he's nearly as good a shot as I am, although he's never, not *once*, beaten me at any of our one-on-one games.

Tim spends a lot of time over at my house shooting hoops and hanging out. He doesn't get along too well with his stepdad, who's an even bigger moron than my old man. I mean, at least my dad isn't a drunk and, for the most part, isn't around. Tim and I never talk much about our families but we don't need to; it's pretty obvious that Tim doesn't like being at his place very much. Also, Tim and my sister have some kind of thing going on—nothing that's any of my business, but they're pretty tight. Cindy thinks I don't know, but why would I care? Tim's no Eddie Farr, so if he likes Cindy, it's cool, although what he sees in her is a mystery to me.

This afternoon, like most afternoons, Tim-bo and I are working out at the hoop in my driveway. I once asked him why he kept playing with me since he *never* won.

He laughed and answered, "Well, someday I'm gonna beat your ass."

I laughed back. "Not in this lifetime."

"Maybe not," he said, "but I'm a better player when I practice with you."

I didn't push it because, in the first place, it was kind of a crummy thing to remind him that I always beat him, and also because Tim's the only guy around who can give me any kind of a workout. He's a good athlete; in addition to hoops, he plays football and baseball like I do. The truth is nobody my age, high-school age, is really much competition for me anymore—that's why college would be so cool, but of course thanks to my old man . . . whatever.

I ask Tim, "So you want first outs?"

"Sure."

"Make it take it?"

Tim shakes his head. "Not with the shooting touch you've had lately. Let's go alternate possessions."

I shrug. "Whatever, Tim-bo. Pick yer poison. I'm feelin' pretty strong."

He laughs. "That's your breath, Paul—or maybe your feet."

I say, "Oh Tim-bo, bad move—now you've insulted me—now all my greatness will be cast before you."

Tim smiles. "Shut up and play."

He takes the ball out and I check it to him. As we start to go at it, we launch into the rhyming rap song from that Tom Hanks movie *Big*, the song the two kids always rap out together; Tim and I always start every workout like this.

Tim dribbles the ball at the top of the key as we rap.

He tries to shoot, but I block his shot and grab the ball.

I laugh and say, "You owe me . . . awwwwwe!"

I make a couple moves, then square up and shoot. Nothing but net.

Tim takes the ball again and says, "My turn, bro, watch and learn."

That day when John-Boy Reich called me bro, it really bugged me, but Tim-bo and I *are* like brothers, and have been since we were ten years old: playing sports together, sleeping over, and watching every movie known to man. We never run out of stuff to slam each other about. There's no reason to feel bad about Tim calling me bro, so I try not to, and on we go.

We had our team practice earlier at school. It's late afternoon now and we're both pretty tired, but that's how I like it best. When it starts to hurt, you have to concentrate harder. Sweat pours down the sides of my face and my chest and back. My thighs burn and my calves feel tight. I love this. It gets pretty intense as we bang away under the rim for rebounds.

Shawn is on the front porch in his wheelchair "watching" us. Right, like he gets what's going on. Why Mom thinks this is some kind of wonderful stimulation for Shawn is beyond me. To be totally honest, it's embarrassing to have him out here. It's embarrassing when Shawn starts yelling "ahhhhh" for no reason; it's embarrassing when he drops a load into his diapers and you can smell him from twenty feet away; it's embarrassing when his drool slides out of his mouth and makes a huge wet spot all down his front. And then I always feel embarrassed to feel embarrassed, guilty and bad that I feel so ashamed of Shawn—somehow all these crappy feelings make me work even harder.

While I'm thinking about Shawn, Tim, who has quick hands, jabs the ball away, stealing it from me. He takes it back to the top of the key and tries to put some moves on me. I jab the ball back, catching a little of Tim's hand, actually his little finger—I can tell I got him because my fingernail dug in and I took a little hunk of his skin with the ball. In a real game I might get called for a foul. I glance at his finger and see the little bloody spot where I gouged him.

As I dribble the ball, I ask, "You wanna foul on that?"

"Just play," Tim says. He's cool: No medevac—no infraction.

I begin to circle around the top of the key, dribbling left-handed, right-handed, back and forth, between my legs and behind my back. I start talking trash: "You can't stop me . . . you know you can't . . ."

"Just play!" Tim snaps. He's breathing pretty hard.

"You tired? You feeling tired, Tim-bo? You need to go take a little nappy-poo?"

Tim really hates trash talk, so that's how I usually mess with him, but today he doesn't bite, he concentrates on the ball, and in spite of being tired, he's moving well. I try to go inside, but he blocks me off great. I fake going in again, get a little separation, and take my jumper.

For some reason, Tim just stops. He doesn't even try to block my shot. From the corner of my eye I see him standing flat-footed, staring over at the front porch of the house.

When I let my shot go, it feels a little off so I follow it, and sure enough it rims out. I grab the board easy, too easy, because Tim doesn't even follow me to the hoop.

"Is Shawn okay?" I hear Tim ask. He's still not looking at me as I put back my rebound for an easy layin.

"What?" I holler.

"Your brother—is he supposed to be like that?"

I look over at the porch and see that Shawn is in the middle of a monster seizure. It's a huge, bad one, saliva pouring out of his mouth, his body shaking all over; he looks terrible. In fact, he's slipped down in his wheelchair, and I can't tell if the purple color of his face is the seizure or his chest strap, which is not around his chest anymore, but around his neck.

He's going to choke to death!

———

CHAPTER EIGHT

I run over and lift Shawn up in his wheelchair so that the strap isn't around his throat. His color doesn't change, so maybe it's his seizure that's making his face so purple. Whatever it is, he looks awful. Even though Shawn is super skinny and real light, when he's in a seizure like now, it's hard to get control of him. He gets totally stiff and jerks around a lot. But this seizure is even worse than normal. The drool on the front of his shirt is much more than usual, disgusting, slimy, and smelly.

Tim, standing a little behind me asks, "Can I help?"

I yell, "Get Mom!"

Tim hurries through the front door, and I hear

him call out, "Lindy!"

Two seconds later she comes running out to the porch, followed by Tim and Cindy.

I keep holding Shawn up so the strap won't get around his neck again. Mom rolls the wheelchair back into the house.

I say, "I guess he slipped down in his chair when his seizure hit, and his strap slipped under his chin."

"What do you mean, the strap 'slipped'?" Mom snaps at me, like I'm to blame.

"Just what I said!" I yell.

Mom always gets like this when Shawn has a seizure, crazy from worry. But I'm mad; I'm still holding Shawn up, and his disgusting drool is all over my neck and shoulder.

Mom raises her voice. "Calm down. . . ."

"YOU calm down!" I yell back.

Cindy bursts into tears. Big deal—she bawls at the drop of a hat.

Mom asks, "Can you tell if he was choking before you got to him?"

I think, That'd be a real tragedy, old Shawn getting brain damaged, but the second I think this, I feel guilty and even madder.

I answer Mom. "I don't know."

Finally, Shawn takes a deep breath. He collapses in my arms; all the rigidity and stiffness disappear, like one of those bounce-back inflatable toys when all the air leaks out. Shawn melts into his wheelchair and passes out or goes to sleep—I'm never sure exactly what happens to him after a seizure, but he always gets real quiet.

"Is he all right?" Cindy asks.

Mom checks Shawn's pulse by feeling his neck and looking closely at his face.

"Is he okay?" Cindy asks again, scared. She leans against Tim and buries her face against his chest. He puts his arms around her.

Mom says, "I think he's all right."

Cindy asks, "Mom, how come his seizures are getting worse?"

Although I've also noticed this lately, I haven't wanted to ask about it—maybe I've been afraid of the answer.

Mom says to Cindy, "I don't know what's wrong with him, honey." Mom's voice sounds incredibly sad, like all her hope is being ripped away from her.

I think, Would it really be all that terrible if Shawn . . . I try to stop these thoughts, but I can't control my selfish brain: What's the point of Shawn's life? Why should he have to suffer like this? Why should we? What the hell does a life like his even matter anyway?

I *hate* myself when I feel like this!

I run out of the house and back out to the driveway. My basketball lies in the yard, and I pick it up. I throw it as hard as I can against the metal backboard. It crashes and bounces straight back to me. I throw it again and again, *crash . . . crash . . . crash*.

After a while I look up and see Tim standing, staring at me.

"You got a problem?" I yell.

Tim doesn't say anything.

I square up toward him and take a couple steps in his direction, and I yell again, "You got a problem?!"

Tim turns and walks away from me, not even looking back.

I holler, "Don't turn your back on me, asshole!"

Tim pauses, turns around, and says, his voice low and calm, "I gotta split, man."

Even though Tim-bo is almost always calm and cool and doesn't like to fight, we went at it once before when we were in eighth grade. He was strong and tough. It took my best effort to beat him, and in the end I didn't really kick his ass—he just quit first. He's much bigger and stronger now. But so am I.

I'd love to deck him! I'd love to hit him as hard as I could, even if I got hit back—*especially* if I got hit back.

Tim starts to walk away again. I think about yelling something more as I watch him moving down the sidewalk. I'm still holding the basketball. It takes all my willpower not to bounce it off the back of his head. I'd give anything to force him to come back and fight.

The thing is, though, somewhere in the back of my mind I already know that I'm not angry with Tim. If he hadn't noticed and said something, maybe Shawn would have choked to death. I'm not mad at Tim—I'm just mad, period. I bounce the basketball hard into the ground and it snaps back up into my hands. I throw it one last time, as hard as I can, at the backboard. *CRASH!*

The ball bounces back toward me, but I don't even grab it; I just let it sail over my shoulder, out into the street. I take a couple deep breaths, then look back at Tim walking away. Finally I go out and grab the ball.

I yell to Tim, "Hey, loser boy, hold up, I'll give you a lift."

Tim turns around and looks back at me.

I say, "Come on, man, I'll take you home, really—I'm chilled."

Half smiling, he walks back toward me.

Man, I feel like I'm going to explode.

CHAPTER NINE

Tim lives only about three quarters of a mile from our place, but since he doesn't have a car, most times after we've had a decent workout, I drive him home.

We're cruising down Fifteenth, a busy street where people normally drive about ten to fifteen miles over the speed limit. I'm taking it easy, though, just driving slowly, when I notice this little girl standing on the street corner with her dog, an ugly little black-and-white mutt on a leash. The girl is maybe a fifth or sixth grader. Anyway, she's standing, waiting to cross, and there's a sign I just passed that reads PEDESTRIAN CROSSING, so I brake. The girl looks up and smiles at me.

She starts to walk out, crossing the street, kind of hurrying so that she can get out of my way and I can get going. I glance in my rearview mirror and I see a bright red Camaro, very hot, nice wax job, dark windows. It's roaring toward the intersection on my left in the passing lane. I mean it's really hauling ass. In a split second I see that the girl isn't looking at the outside lane, she hasn't seen the other car—she's actually being pulled by her ugly dog, running toward the path of the Camaro.

It's like time speeds up and slows down both at once. I can see what's going to happen, like it's slow motion, but what can I do? My adrenaline kicks in and I do the only thing I can think of—I lay on my horn.

Tim jumps in his seat. "Shit!"

The little girl jumps too and gives a violent tug on the leash so that her dog jerks backward. A second later, with my horn still blasting, the Camaro roars through where the little girl and the dog would have been if I hadn't startled them. My adrenaline is through the roof, so even after the danger is done, I don't take my hand off the horn right away.

Tim says, "That kid almost bought it."

I stupidly say, "Her dog, too."

But now there's an incredibly loud screeching as the Camaro whips over to the side of the road. Blue smoke pours off the rear tires as his brakes lock. When he comes to a stop, suddenly this arm comes out of the window and he flips me off. He just sits there, giving me the middle finger salute.

Tim says, "Take it easy, Paul."

But it's too late.

The little girl and her lucky mutt jog away down the street as I stick my hand out the window and return the gesture to the Camaro driver. I ease my Honda over to the sidewalk. It's only been about ten minutes since I wanted to fight Tim; this moment is like a dream come true.

The Camaro driver's door opens, and out steps this really big, buff guy, about mid-twenties and tall, maybe six four or six five. He's wearing a tight T-shirt and sweatpants, like he's fresh out of a yuppie gym somewhere. He's blond and smirking with a silly-ass muscleman walk.

Tim, seeing how big he is, says, "Uh-oh."

I glance over at Tim and smile. I feel great.

I open my car door and bound out, like a coiled spring unwinding.

The Camaro guy and I walk toward each other. He outweighs me by probably thirty or forty pounds. He has the kind of physique that you get only from wanting to look like that, sculpted and perfect. His clothes make me sick, his face makes me sick, he's the kind of guy who always stares at Shawn whenever our family goes anyplace, stares and smirks and thinks he's better.

He yells, "You got a problem?"

I smile at him. "Were you tryin' to kill that girl and her dog?"

He says sarcastically, "She's not gonna live much longer anyway if she doesn't start watchin' where she's going."

I smile and say, "That's a pedestrian crossing, and you almost killed her, dickhead."

We're pretty close to each other by now. We've both stepped out of the street, up onto a little green band between the cement sidewalk and the curb, just enough room for a nice fight.

"Screw yourself," he says.

I answer, "Screw myself? How would I do that? Tell me, 'cause you look like you've had some practice."

He gets a funny look in his eyes, not fear, more

like surprise. I can see by his expression that people *never* stand up to him. He's a bully and he likes it, just like every bully in the world.

"What'd you say?" he asks, sticking his big chest out and clenching his fists like that's going to scare me.

I burst out laughing and answer, "You heard me, sweetie." Man, I'm looking forward to this. "I said that you probably screw yourself every chance you get."

His face flushes bright red, another good sign—nobody ever fights decent when they're running on pure anger. He spits and stammers. "You . . . I . . . ."

I laugh again.

Now we're standing right in front of each other. He's a full head taller than me, which annoys me. I hate big guys who think they're big men.

I say, "You know what, asshole? I can tell you work out real hard to look like you do. You must be proud of yourself. You're so cute that I'm not even gonna hit you in the face. I'm not even gonna mark you up. I want you to stay pretty and sweet for—"

Suddenly he takes an awkward swing at me and lets out a loud grunt. Probably half his energy just went into this one punch. He misses me by a foot even though I barely move. He'd have missed me anyway.

I feel good, totally ready. This guy is everything wrong with the world . . . everything wrong with *my* world.

I say, "Is that all you got? Do I need to stand a little more still for you?"

He cocks back his left hand and telegraphs his swing from about a mile away. Just before the punch arrives, I move a little so that I can take it high up, on the side of my head. I hear his fingers crack on contact and watch him wince. I've got a really hard skull, and besides, when I'm in a fight, I never feel a punch anyway; in fact, this feels like he just brushed me with a feather duster. I always need to get hit, though; it's always the final piece for me.

I launch a combination of punches into his gut. The first is a hard right that pretty much takes all his wind. The next two, a left and another right, are even harder than the first. He drops to his knees, wheezing for breath, but before he can recover, I kick him in his right kidney. I'm still wearing soft-toed basketball shoes, so I bend my foot like I'm kicking a soccer ball and it really digs in; he'll be pissing blood for a week. He rolls over onto his back, gasping for air, covering his head. I stomp his chest, then I bend over and lay three hard, straight rights into his ribs.

He rolls onto his side and vomits. I circle around behind him and pause. It's like I don't even see him anymore—what I see is my brother's seizure, wanting to fight Tim, my piece-of-slime dad.

I get ready to kick him in his lower back. This kick will bruise his spine and finish him off—

Suddenly arms wrap around me and pull me down from behind. As I'm falling, I look over at the guy on the ground and see the fear in his eyes.

I hear a voice. "That's it, man, he's had enough."

At first I don't even know who's talking to me or what he's talking about. I struggle to break loose, but whoever is holding me has a good grip.

"Stop it, Paul, he's had it."

My head clears and I start to notice the grass, the street, the sounds of cars passing by. Tim has grabbed me. I feel the rage rise up again, ready to fight him too.

But Tim says, "Come on, please, stop, before you go too far."

His voice sounds afraid, and as fast as I've slid into my combat mode, I slide back out again.

I notice more of everything around me—the

back of the Camaro, the wires overhead, a scrap of paper blowing along the sidewalk.

Finally I say, "Okay," real softly. I hardly even recognize the sound of my own voice.

"I'm okay," I say again.

Tim says, "You sure?" still holding me back.

I say, "Yeah, I'm sure."

Tim lets me go.

The guy on the ground lies there holding his side, half leaning up on one elbow.

"Who . . ." he starts to ask, then winces. His eyes have that beaten look, scared and hurt and even though I never touched his face, it's red and scraped-up from rubbing on the ground.

"Who . . . are . . . you?" he mutters.

I stare at him and don't say anything for a couple seconds; then I answer him, real smart-ass: "I'm my brother's keeper." I pause a second, then say, deadpan, "And I'm an excellent driver." This last line is from the movie *Rain Man*, about these two brothers, Tom Cruise and that Dustin guy who's autistic.

I say, "You got any other questions, ass wipe?" hoping he'll say something stupid, hoping he'll say *anything*.

Tim grabs my arm, but I jerk it loose.

"Sorry," Tim says quickly, but then, "Let's get out of here, okay, before the cops come."

I look once more at Mr. Red Camaro Buff Boy. He doesn't say anything, but I notice that there's a big wet spot on the front of his sweatpants. For half a second I actually feel sorry for him.

In the car again Tim stares out the front and is real quiet.

"What?" I ask him, already knowing what he's going to say.

Tim answers, "You coulda killed that guy. One day you're going to go too far."

I know he's right. A sick feeling rushes through me and I know he's right. I just don't know how to stop it.

I say, "You don't understand."

Tim stares at me for a few seconds without saying anything, then finally answers real softly, "Yeah I do."

I'm not sure what he means, and I'd like to say something back, but I can't think what else to say, so we just drive in silence.

CHAPTER TEN

I pull up to Tim's house to drop him off. To be honest, his place is kind of a dump. On Queen Anne Hill the view houses like ours are really expensive, high-end cribs, but some of the old, old houses like Tim's are actually run-down, cruddy-looking rentals. I've noticed that Tim never looks over at me when we pull up in front of his place. He always hops out of the car real quick, like now. I think he's embarrassed not only by what a cracker box he lives in, but by the crap that happens inside too, like with his stepdad.

"Peace," Tim says, not looking at me, as he closes the car door.

I answer, "Later."

• • •

Back home, as I come through the front door, Mom calls, "Paul?"

I answer, "Yeah."

"Are you okay, sweetie?" she asks, walking up to me from the kitchen and hugging me.

"I'm fine."

"You sure?"

Mom feels guilty for acting nutty when Shawn was having his seizure. This happens all the time.

I say, "Really, Mom, I'm fine. How's Shawn?"

Cindy walks in and answers my question. "He's asleep. But his seizure was really bad."

I say, "I know."

I notice that my knuckles are bright red from hitting the Camaro guy. I kind of hide them behind my back.

Mom's forehead gets all wrinkled and her face suddenly looks about a thousand years old. "His seizures *are* getting worse."

I don't say anything. The truth is I feel numb. This is why fighting feels so good to me: After I've let out all my anger, there's always this numbness, a calm feeling—I don't know how to describe it.

Cindy says, "Mom and Dad are going to take

Shawn to the doctor."

I say, "Yeah? Good."

I don't even know if I mean it. The doctors have never helped Shawn, never helped any of us. What's the point? But of course I don't say this. I just stand here and try not to worry. I don't know what else to do, so I let the numbness take me away.

This is my life, our lives. This is what being around Shawn means. No matter what else happens outside, there's always Shawn, always his seizures, always another useless doctor, always . . . everything about him. At times I even get why Dad left. Of course, getting it doesn't mean forgiving.

It's been three days since Shawn's seizure on the porch.

Mom and Dad took Shawn to see his neurologist (brain doctor), and I guess the doc adjusted Shawn's drugs. Maybe that's helped a little bit. Shawn's still having a lot of seizures, but they aren't quite so intense. They definitely aren't as bad as that one he had on the porch. A lot of the time I try not to think about Shawn at all, try not to worry about him or feel sorry for him or feel sorry for myself because of him. Most times my feelings about Shawn are so confused, I wish that he'd just . . . I don't know . . . that he would just go ahead and . . . I don't know . . .

I'm up in my room when I hear Mom call up the stairs. She wants Cindy and me to go down. When we get there, Mom says, "I need to tell you guys something." She stops, like she doesn't know how to say it. "I need to discuss something with you guys," she tries again.

"You said that," I say to her. I wonder what we've done . . . she looks serious.

But she says to us, "You're not in trouble. I just have to tell you something."

"What's going on?" Cindy asks. She sounds suspicious.

"It's about your dad," Mom answers.

I groan. "Now what?"

"I haven't even told you what it's about," Mom snaps. But I don't let her finish.

"If it has to do with Dad, you don't have to," I snap back at her. I go sit on the couch, and Cindy sits next to me. I can tell she wants to hear what Mom has to say. Cindy is such a dork. Maybe I should just let Eddie Farr have her; they could raise a nice little family of total imbeciles. Actually, Cindy isn't like Eddie. In fact, as goofy as she acts a lot of the time, she's smart at school stuff; she just doesn't have any common sense.

Mom interrupts my thoughts. "You're mad at your dad. I know that, but you need to set that aside for a moment and just listen. *The Alice Ponds Show* is going to do a program about your dad's newest project—"

Cindy interrupts. "The thing about the schools?"

"No," Mom says.

"What new project?" I ask.

"Your dad's writing a new book. It's about Earl Detraux."

"Oh no!" Cindy moans and curls up on the couch. I can see she's really upset.

I say, "Who? Who's Earl Dayglow?"

"Has Dad gone crazy?" Cindy asks from behind her knees.

"Your dad thinks it's an important story. He thinks—" Mom starts to answer. But Cindy interrupts her. I can tell this whole Earl guy thing is something bad.

So I ask again, "What's going on?! Who's this Earl guy?"

"He's that monster from eastern Washington who murdered his kid," Cindy hisses.

I still don't know what they're talking about, but as they go on, I catch the drift. I guess this Detraux guy killed his retarded kid and got sent to prison. I'm still not tracking real close, though, so I say, "I don't get it. Why's Dad into that?" Mom gives me this whole bull story about how Dad's writing is all about getting other people to understand what it's like for families like ours—who have kids like Shawn. Yeah, like he'd know anything about that. I start to get really pissed off again in time to hear her say, "He wants you both to know that if you want to, you can join him on the program and talk about life with your brother. The people at *The Alice Ponds Show*—"

I can't believe this! *The Alice Ponds Show* is one of those I-married-my-sister-who's-in-love-with-our-cousin's-Pomeranian types of programs. I yell, "Right! Alice Ponds. I'd rather have ground glass pounded up my nose!"

"Paul," Mom starts.

But Cindy interrupts, "Join him? Why?"

Mom makes this big excuse about Dad thinking he's going to help people by going on the show . . . blah, blah, blah . . . it's all bull, of course; after all, my dad's behind it.

Mom goes on to say, "Your father—"

I interrupt. "My father is a hopeless jerk, and I wouldn't help him do *anything*, least of all go on a freak show and talk about my brother." I pause for a second and glance over at poor idiot Shawn sitting there drooling. Thank God he doesn't know what a complete and total ass our old man is. "Alice Ponds?" I say, unable to believe that even Dad could stoop this low. "Alice Friggin' Ponds!"

I feel a huge rush of anger. Now the whole country is going to see my brother, the whole world is going to look at him and feel sorry for him and for my dad, but nobody's going to *really* know the truth. I have no idea what goes on in Shawn's head, and he has no idea that I even exist! But millions of people are going to have the totally wrong idea that they *know* us: "Do you ever talk to your brother?" "Does your brother like to be read to?" "Does your brother like Christmas? Easter eggs?" "What's his favorite TV show?" "How does your brother communicate his feelings to you?" "If you could have one wish come true for your brother, what would it be?"

My brother this and my brother that! Hell, I barely even *have* a brother!

Good job, Dad. Just friggin' great!

CHAPTER ELEVEN

Unbelievably, my brain-dead sister actually decided to accompany Dickhead Dad to L.A. for *The Alice Ponds Show*. They taped the program a couple days ago and it's showing this afternoon. The gods have seen fit to torture me, meaning that by an utter fluke of horrible luck, I don't have basketball practice today. So when I get home from school, there's Mom and Shawn and Cindy all parked in front of the TV, and guess what's coming on in about five minutes? Yep, good old *Alice Ponds*. I'm stuck without any decent excuse for not watching. It's ridiculous, all of us curled up nice and cozy to watch this total catastrophe of total garbage!

I look at Shawn. For once I'm glad that he's so out of it. How horrible it would be to have your sole function in life be a prop in your own father's "artistic" pity party? Disgusting.

The show starts and it's all the usual crap. Alice Ponds is a total phony.

I'm not paying much attention, really. Alice says something and Dad says something back and all the morons in the audience, who make Eddie Farr look like Albert Einstein, start asking totally stupid questions. It's hard to believe that this show could actually be as bad as I thought it would be, but it's *worse*.

I walk over to the kitchen and grab a handful of potato chips. As I walk back toward the couch, I notice that Mom isn't looking so I slip Shawn a little piece of chip, laying it on his tongue. I have no idea whether Shawn likes this or not, but it's a little ritual we have going. Whenever I can, I feed Shawn bits of stuff he wouldn't get otherwise. His regular diet is oatmeal and mashed-up eggs and other nasty stuff that nobody should have to eat, but Shawn can't swallow very well and this soft food is easier on him. Can you imagine being too messed up to swallow? When he eats, he drools even more than normal, so Mom has this huge bib she puts on him. The bib catches the drool and all the food that slips back out of his mouth when he's being fed. Mom hates for him to eat without his bib, which I can understand, but I don't care— some food pleasures are just too good to pass up. So when Mom isn't looking, I slip my bro treats.

To be honest, most of the time it's hard to know how to be good to Shawn. I know it's totally weak to feel this, but nobody understands unless they have a brother or sister like Shawn themselves. There're kids at school who volunteer for one week- end a year to help out at the Special Olympics. For me, these kids are the worst, always talking about how cool retarded kids are—like they really know what it's like to be around a human veg twenty-four seven. And another thing, in our family we're all supposed to act like Shawn's condition isn't any big deal. We never talk about it, and it's obvious that Mom wants us to just accept him. I try to do this, but when I have a friend over and we walk into a room and it smells like shit, I mean literally like feces because fourteen-year-old Shawn has just taken a big dump in his pants—it's kind of hard to pretend that everything is normal family life. I try to love Shawn, and most of the time I do, but sometimes it's too hard. So one of the ways I let Shawn know that I care about him is to sneak him bits of tasty stuff when Mom isn't watching, just in case somewhere inside himself, he knows I'm his brother.

Over the years I've introduced Shawn to the joys of Wheat Thins, smoked oysters, strawberry cheesecake, the full range of Frito-Lay products, and an occasional frosty sip of a tall Bud and a wide variety of other fine malt beverages, both domestic and imported (I think he's partial to Coors Light). Hey, the guy's gotta have some fun!

Right now, he's sucking away on the hunk of Mesquite Barbecue potato chip that I just slipped him. As I cruise back to the couch for more Alice Ponds torture, I wink at Shawn, as if he knew what was going on.

I try to watch and listen: Blah, blah, blah . . . blah, blah, blah . . . and then a little more, blah, blah, blah.

Just as Dad and Cindy come on, Shawn goes into a seizure. Mom looks at him and jumps up, hurrying over to make sure he's okay, that his strap is snug around his chest. As she stands next to him, she runs her hand through his hair, real gentle, trying to reassure him. My mom is the best. I can't help but wonder whether the bite of chip I gave Shawn is going to cause a problem, but luckily he's not choking.

After a couple seconds Shawn falls asleep or whatever it is that happens to him once the electric currents in his brain stop misfiring. I wonder if he's dreaming. Can a guy with a totally useless brain, a brain that can't even think, dream? I've seen dogs and cats having dreams; you'd think that if even animals do it, a human brain, even a bad one, would have *something* going on. I try to shake off these thoughts; they don't help anything.

With Shawn sleeping, Mom sits back down and we watch as Dad's interview comes on. In the videotape Detraux is in prison and Dad's sitting there with him and they talk about how Earl killed his little two-year-old retarded kid. It's kind of interesting: the gray prison bars, the guards standing around in the background, the big cuffs on Detraux's hands. Earl looks sad, and Dad has this phony-looking sympathetic expression. What I like best is seeing my old man in "the big house"—if the world was fair at all, guys who run out on their retarded kids would get life plus twenty years.

After they play the interview, a woman in the audience asks Cindy, "Do you wanna kill your bruvver?"

Cindy, without missing a beat, asks back, "Which brother?"

I burst out laughing, and the real Cindy, sitting next to me on the couch, blushes and smiles. We give each other high fives.

On TV Cindy answers the woman's question. "No, I've never thought about doing anything like that. But I have thought about Shawn's life, about how his condition affects all of us. I mean, I've heard some people talk about what a 'precious gift' a retarded child is to a family—but I think that's totally a lie, an excuse to deal with how heartbreaking and hard it can be sometimes."

Alice Ponds, real condescending and like she's speaking to a five-year-old, asks Cindy, "Surely you're not for mercy killing of innocent children who have hurt brains?"

Cindy answers, "Surely you don't speak from any experience of living with a severely handicapped brother or sister?"

Alice sputters. "Well no, I don't have any first-hand experience of a sibling with—"

Cindy interrupts, "No, I didn't think so, because if you had, you wouldn't ask that question. Mercy killing? No, I've never thought about killing Shawn; none of us know what his life is really like. But I have thought, lots of times, about him dying. And I've wondered, a million times, what the purpose of his life is. There's no way I'll ever believe that the problems a brother like Shawn brings to a family are 'gifts from God.' That's the stupidest thing in the world and the worst kind of denial. Having Shawn as a brother is hard. You even feel guilty for feeling bad about it."

I'm sitting here amazed. Cindy sounds so smart. She's putting into words all kinds of stuff I've thought but could never say. I'm afraid to look over at Mom, but when I peek, she looks quiet, sad, but not mad at all.

We *never* talk about Shawn this way. We *never* tell the truth: that Mom has sacrificed her whole life to take care of him; that Cindy does the same thing. Cindy's got friends and is into music a little, but her life is pretty much committed to Shawn too. And then there's me. I'm trapped here taking care of everyone, trying to protect everyone, especially my brother. All of us give our lives away, every day, for Shawn. All of us except my dad.

As the show ends, Mom leaves the room, turning her face away so that Cindy and I won't see the tears in her eyes.

I say to Cindy, softly so that Mom won't hear us, "You were great on the show. The things you said about how Shawn's condition affected us all, how it changed us forever, that was such a great way to put it."

Cindy and I talk back and forth, being sure to speak softly so that Mom won't hear.

Suddenly Cindy asks whether I think Dad might be planning on hurting Shawn. At first I don't even know what she's talking about, but then she explains: What about all the stuff about Detraux? What about Dad talking about killing your kid to end his pain? Cindy's worried about it.

"Nah, Shawn's safe," I say.

I think about it and add, kind of lamely, hoping I sound more sure of myself than I actually feel,

"Yeah, Shawn's safe. Even if Dad's gone nuts and wants to do something, he'd have to come through me."

Cindy nods and looks away.

But now something shifts inside me. It hits me hard. I feel my face go red and my hands start to shake. I'm totally ashamed. I flash back to that day I beat up the bullies who were hurting Shawn with the Bic lighter. I know Cindy is probably thinking about that day too. But she doesn't know the *whole* story. She doesn't know what really happened— nobody does. Cindy thinks I saved Shawn, and I guess maybe I did save him, but . . .

I take a couple deep breaths to try and get control of myself.

Could Dad be thinking of killing Shawn? I know what Cindy's asking. We all have moments when we wonder what Shawn's life means. We all have moments when we wonder what life would be like if Shawn weren't around. I feel kind of sick thinking about this, especially thinking about my dad. Could Dad be thinking about mercy-killing Shawn? I guess he *could* be.

But why would he? After all, Dad's Shawn lives only in the books Dad writes. Dad's Shawn never needs his diaper changed. Dad's Shawn never needs to be fed, or has a seizure, or needs protection from bullies. Only Dad has escaped the *real* Shawn. The rest of us, Shawn especially, are like Earl Detraux, stuck right here in our own jails forever and never going anywhere.

CHAPTER TWELVE

I'm sure that the main reason I decided to come along with Dad and Cindy and Shawn today is the chance to watch my dad suffer. It really is obvious that it's hard on him to be around Shawn, and today that's exactly where he is! I'm gonna love this; welcome to my world, Dad!

Dad's taking the three of us, Shawn, Cindy, and me, to the Seattle Center, a repeat of a trip we took years ago, back when I was in sixth grade. What's funny about this, a sick, disturbed, totally messed-up "funny," is that Mom isn't here this time to play the buffer between Shawn and Dad. Of course, he's got Cindy, who is a Mom clone when it comes to caring for Shawn, but at least Dad will have to take

74

some responsibility. I can't stop wondering, Why is Dad doing this? What does Dad want? It's like he's trying to be a parent again, but I know that can't be true.

As we drive toward the Seattle Center, Dad's trying to be all cheerful, which is ridiculous. He's singing along to songs on the radio's oldies station, like "Lola" by the Kinks. When we were little, we used to go for rides in the car and sing "Lola," so Dad is cheerleading us to sing along now.

It's totally ridiculous.

Cindy actually seems to be *enjoying* it! I swear, sometimes she acts more retarded than Shawn. She's singing away, happy as can be. Shawn is moaning his loud "ahhhhhhhh," which is not exactly in whatever key Cindy and Dad are singing in.

Dad says, "Come on, Pauly—jump in anywhere," then starts to sing again.

He has a really rat-sphincter voice, too.

We get to the Seattle Center and Dad unloads Shawn's wheelchair, lifts him out of the van, and straps him onto the leather wheelchair seat. We head toward the amusement park rides. I hear people screaming and laughing as we get closer, the roar of the roller coaster and the tinkling sound of the merry-go-round. The smells of popcorn and junk food are doing combat with the stink of diesel fumes wafting through the air. There's a pretty decent size crowd.

As we're walking, getting closer to the ticket stand, a guy about my age walks by in the opposite direction. The guy looks at Cindy and she glances back at him. He's an okay-looking guy, a little on the preppy side, but even I notice him checking out Cindy.

Dad sees this too and smiles. He says to Cindy, "You think he was checking you out or just gaping at Shawn?"

Cindy's face drops, and I can tell that her feelings are hurt. She gives Dad a killer look.

Dad tries to cover. "I was just kidding, sweetheart. Of course he was . . ."

But before Dad can finish, Cindy spins and walks away. Dad awkwardly turns Shawn's wheelchair around so he can take off after her.

"Idiot," I say under my breath—and I'm not talking about my brother!

I wait, staying out of it. Dad catches up to Cindy and talks to her, no doubt trying to talk his way out of trouble, trying to charm her like he does everybody else, all the time. In a couple minutes they come back, and Dad, looking at our faces, laughs and says, "Lighten up. This is going to be great!"

Shawn starts to rock back and forth in his chair, going "ahhhhhh" even louder than normal. There's so much noise and confusion and chaos here that it must be kind of weird for him.

I say, "You know, maybe this was a mistake—to bring Shawn."

Dad says, "Nonsense. There are plenty of things for Shawn and me to do."

Shawn and him? I can't believe what I'm hearing, but Dad fishes into his wallet and digs out two fifty-dollar bills, handing one to me and one to Cindy.

Dad glances at his watch and says, "We'll meet you guys back here in, say, a couple hours. Two o'clock all right?"

I don't believe this! Dad alone with Shawn for two whole hours? Perfect! Before he can change his mind or say another word, I say, "Yeah, great, all right." I grab Cindy's arm, and before she can protest, we're gone.

• • •

The two hours go by pretty fast, a few rides, a few arcade games—but all the time, in the back of my mind, I keep wondering how Shawn and Dad are doing.

Cindy and I are back at the meeting spot only a few minutes late. Of course, there's no sign of Shawn or Dad. We stand around not saying anything for a while. Finally she asks, "He said two hours, right?"

I answer, "Yeah," even though I know she already knows the answer.

Cindy decides to go spend the last two bucks of her fifty on something to eat (my cash was gone in about ten minutes).

While Cindy searches for fat enhancers, there's this big fountain near where I'm standing, close to where we're supposed to meet Shawn and Dad. I sit on the edge of it and wait, keeping cool, or at least trying to. I can't help but be a little mad at Dad for being late. Of course, I don't know what's up with him and Shawn; still, it's typical that he'd be thoughtless about the time.

Finally, after another five minutes or so, I see Dad and Shawn working their way through the crowd toward me. A few seconds later Cindy shows up too, carrying a huge wad of blue cotton candy.

"Nice sugar," I say to her, ignoring Dad.

"You're just jealous," she says.

Actually, even though her blue lips are gross, she's right—I'd love a hit off her tooth decay on a stick.

I finally glance over at Dad. I can only imagine how it must have been to push old Shawn around in his wheelchair through the crowds and over the rutted, crumbling surface of these grounds for two hours plus. Dad's face is red and his hair, what's left of it, is all messed up. He really looks hacked out. Good—serves him right.

I can't resist. "So Dad, did you guys have a good time?"

Dad glances back at me like he doesn't even understand my question.

Back in the parking lot at the van, Dad puts Shawn into the passenger side in back, belting him in. Cindy and I get in too. I'm up front riding shotgun, and Cindy's next to Shawn, sitting right behind Dad.

We start to head out, and right away Shawn starts to moan "ahhhhhhh" even louder than he usually does.

After a few minutes, Dad slams his hand on the dashboard and yells, "Damnit!"

Cindy says, "I know. He gets a little intense, doesn't he?"

Dad says, "Yeah, 'intense' is one word for it!"

I look at Dad, and his face is even redder than before—he looks totally burned out and totally stressed. I almost feel sorry for him. Almost. But if anybody in the world deserves to have to put in some time with Shawn's noise, it's dear old Dick-head Dad.

Suddenly Shawn goes "AHHHHHHHHH!" louder than before.

Dad jumps and says, "Damn, Shawn."

I say to Dad, pretty low and calm, "He can't help it."

Dad says, not even looking at me, "Yeah, I know. I just can't stand to hear him in pain."

Dad's squeezing the steering wheel really hard; his knuckles are white. The traffic is heavy. Cars are jammed bumper to bumper and it's hot out. Despite the air-conditioning all of us are sweaty and tired.

I ask Dad, "How do you know Shawn's in pain?"

"For God's sake, Paul, listen to him. Does it

sound to you like he's enjoying himself?"

Shawn yells "AHHHHHHHHH" again.

I say to Dad, "He's like this all the time. You're just not around to hear it."

"No, he's not like this *all* the time!" Dad snaps at me.

I glance at Dad for half a second and see that he's giving me this real sincere, serious stare, so I look away from him. I just stare out the windshield at all the exhaust fumes and the hot sun reflecting off the windows and chrome of the cars ahead of us.

Cindy says, "You're right, Dad, Shawn doesn't do this all the time, he's just—"

Shawn interrupts, almost screaming now. "AHHHHHHHHHHHHHH."

I almost laugh, but I suddenly notice that Dad is looking in the rearview mirror at Cindy; he doesn't see that the traffic has stopped.

I yell, "LOOK OUT!!!"

Dad sees what's happening and slams on his brakes. He screeches to within a few inches of a blue Ford truck in front of us. We all bounce forward, jerking violently, then fly back into our seats.

Dad quickly looks back at Cindy and Shawn.

"Are you guys all right?"

Cindy says, "Yeah, I'm okay."

Dad looks over at me but I don't say anything; I don't even look at him.

Cindy says, "Shawn's okay too."

Suddenly a huge mouthful of drool slips out of Shawn's lips, down over his chin onto his shirt. Dad sort of snorts and says, "Yeah, he looks just great . . . terrific. Cindy, can you please quiet him down?"

Cindy says, "Dad, you know I can't."

Dad says, "Yeah, I know, I'm sorry."

As if on cue Shawn belts out, "AHHHHHH," then "AHHHHHH, AHHHHHH, AHHHHHH."

Dad says, "He's driving me crazy!"

I can't help myself, I can't stop the words from coming out of my mouth; I say, "He's just your kid, Dad, the fruit of your loins, your beloved son, your—"

Dad interrupts, not even looking at me, "Please, Paul, don't, I can't stand it now—"

"AHHHH, AHHHH, AHHHH."

Suddenly Shawn begins to make a familiar gagging sound, gasping as he slides into a seizure. Saliva pours out of his mouth, and his body twists and turns in a tortured rush of spasms.

I say to Dad, "YOU can't stand it, huh? What about Shawn?"

The rest of the ride back to our house, where Dad can drop us off and then run away again, is quiet. Shawn has passed out and Cindy's eyes are brimming with tears. As the traffic thins, Dad seems to relax a little bit. I don't.

I've never wanted more to hit him than I do right now.

CHAPTER THIRTEEN

Dad whips the van into the driveway and comes to a bumpy stop. He jumps out and slams the door. I do the same thing, making sure to slam my door at least as hard and loud as he did. I start to walk toward the house.

I assume that Dad's getting Shawn's chair or maybe getting Shawn himself out of the van, but suddenly I feel a strong grip on my shoulder, too strong for Cindy's hand. I jerk my body hard and the hand loses its grip.

Dad yells, "Hey!"

But suddenly something totally bizarre happens inside me, something weird and completely foreign. Normally, if you grabbed me the way Dad just did, in the mood that I'm in right now, you'd be crawling around picking up your teeth. But that's just it: I don't hit him. It's utter weirdness; I can't even describe it. I'm not afraid of him—at least I don't think it's fear. I don't know what it is, but a rush of words and feelings pounds through my brain and down into my throat.

I yell, "I hate you! I really, really hate you!" I pause a second, then add, "You only think about yourself!"

I've never said this to him before, not so straight up like this.

Dad, looking furious, starts to answer. "What!? Pauly—"

I interrupt. "You want this big, perfect, totally bullshit family!"

"Watch your mouth!" Dad says.

I yell, "You watch it for me . . . that'd be as close as you've ever been to being a parent!"

Dad, his face full of anger, steps toward me, getting right into my face.

Without thinking about it, without even knowing I'm going to do it, I take a small step back. I've never backed down from anybody in my whole life! I don't get it. I'm not scared of him . . . it's just . . .

I don't know what's happening.

What the hell am I doing? I hate him! This is my chance to finally nail him. But something inside holds me back, freezes me.

Cindy, standing back at the van, starts to cry— she looks terrified. She probably thinks I'm going to kill her daddy, but I can't move a muscle—it's like I'm paralyzed.

Dad's so mad he can't even talk. He starts to stammer. "I . . . you . . ."

I interrupt, yelling, "I'm getting as far away from you as I possibly can."

Dad asks, "Pauly, what're you talking about?"

I stare into his eyes the whole time; our faces are only inches apart. I scream, "I'm talking about an athletic scholarship, a full ride, somewhere where I'll never see you again! As soon as I can, I'm getting the hell out of here and away from you!" This is all bull, of course. I can't leave Mom and Cindy and Shawn, I know I can't, but I say it anyway just to hurt Dad.

Dad looks like somebody just slapped his face. He steps back from me and drops his eyes to the ground. His lips quiver a little and he takes a deep breath. Finally, his voice calm and soft, he says,

"That's fine, Pauly, that's what you *should* do, but what do you want from me, huh, what do you want me to do?"

I don't hesitate. "Get out of my life!" I yell. I think about how trapped I am, how hopeless I feel. "And don't ever, EVER show your face at any of my games again, okay? Can you get over yourself enough to do that? To just get the hell out of my life!"

Dad steps back from me, almost stumbling. He mumbles, "You got it."

I yell, "GOOD!"

But the weirdness keeps rushing through me; I'm not afraid, I'm not even angry. I can't tell what it is that I'm feeling until a few seconds pass. Now it hits me—I'm incredibly *sad*. My chest aches and my head throbs and my stomach turns over. My skin is tingling, and I feel like I felt when I was a little kid and something terrible happened and I couldn't do anything about it. I feel like I felt when I first understood, first really *got it*, that my brother was never going to be okay, that my brother was always going to be . . . totally messed up.

I glance back at the van and see that Shawn is still sound asleep. Shawn. My brother . . . my . . . suddenly a rush of tears is ready to explode out of me.

Not wanting Dad to see me cry, I turn away from him and run into the house. Mom is standing on the porch, staring at us, her mouth open and a look of shock covering her face. I rush past her, turning away so that she won't see my tears either. I race up the stairs to my room.

I slam my bedroom door behind me and sit on my bed. At least Dad knows how I feel now; at least I've finally told him what I think of him. I spot my basketball lying on the floor, pick it up, and begin spinning it in my hands. I take deep breaths, trying to calm down, but I still have that little-kid feeling of being tense and helpless and sad.

I'm glad we've got a game to play tomorrow night. I'm going to play harder than I've ever played. Somehow this game is going to be for Shawn, and somehow I'm going to make him proud of me, whether he knows he is or not. Hell, that doesn't even make any sense! How can someone feel proud when they don't have a brain?

I hear words inside my head saying, Shawn, all of this is happening because of you; I'm trying to live my life, but how can I do that when you don't have one?

I feel insane. I think maybe I am!

* * *

Mom comes to my room after Dad leaves. Her face is red. I can't tell if she's mad or scared.

She asks, "What was that about?"

"I don't know."

"Well, you better figure it out, Paul. Your father is—"

I interrupt her. "My father is a total jerk. Period. End of story."

Mom says, a sharper tone to her voice, "Your father is doing his best."

I laugh. "Come on. That's ridiculous, especially coming from you. Dad's a total asshole. He left us, abandoned Shawn. He thinks that by sending us money, he's doing something."

Mom says, her voice calm, "It's not that simple, honey. But never mind that. The fact is, you've got to get a handle on your temper before something terrible happens. I thought you and your dad were actually going to hit each other."

I don't tell Mom how much I *wanted* to hit him, how much I wanted to *kill* him but how I couldn't do it. How can I explain it to her when I don't even understand it myself?

I say, "I know what you're saying about my

temper, I know what you mean. You don't need to worry about me—I'll figure it out."

Mom says softly, "You better figure it out soon, Paul. Something's hurting you and making you hurt others. I'm here for you if you need to talk; I'm *your* mother too, you know, not just Shawn's. Remember that, okay?"

Mom leaves my room, closing the door quietly behind her.

I feel sick inside, crazy and hopeless—I need to escape. Maybe not like Dad, leaving everyone behind forever; I know that's not possible.

But I definitely need to find some way to run away from these crazy thoughts and feelings or I *am* going to go crazy—crazy or to jail.

CHAPTER FOURTEEN

Itz Friday nite and I'm totally shh-faceshd . . . I mean "f a c e d" totally shh-f a c e d . . . been pounding Southern Comfort and Coke-a-Colsha . . . I mean . . .

"*Cola . . . coooo . . . coooo . . . coooo . . . co-laaaaa . . .*"

Tim-bo saysh to me, "What're you shingin?"

Shh, man, he's even drunker than I amz. I start to laugh "Ha-ha-ha-ha-ha . . ." Itsh so weird, like I can hear my laughfshs echoing in my brain. . . . My lipz feel all tingling, and shh . . . this makesh me laugh even more . . . Ha-ha-ha-ha-ha.

I'm sooooooo way-shted . . . I mean "w a s t e d."

I probably shouldn't be driving right now, but I'm too drunk to walk . . . ha-ha-ha-ha-ha-ha-ha-ha . . .

Tim saysh, "We totally kick'd ash tonite."

He musht mean our bashketball game. We won sheventy-ate . . . I mean s e v e n t y - e i g h t . . . 78 . . . to 42 . . . f o r t y - t w o !! I shcored thirty-two pointsh . . .

"Yesh we did Tim-o-phy, my fine young can-nibull . . . ha-ha-ha-ha-ha."

All of a shudden, Tim shtarts to cry.

"Whasht wrong, Tim-bo?" I ashk my old pal and my t e a m m a t e .

Tim saysh, "I'm never going to leave this plashe."

"Whatdaya mean, amigoooo?" I ashk Tim back. He'sh cryin' bad, big tears and shnot outa his nosh. . . .

"I can't ever leave my momz," Tim saysh.

Even thru my buzzzzz I hear dat-shh . . . I feel the tears start to come to my eyesh too . . . I can't leave eve-er, eth-er . . . I mean e v e r , e i t h e r .

We're heading down Fifteenth again, the shtreet were I kicked that Camaro guy's ash. . . . We're driving right by the shpot . . . jus' drivin' and drivin'. . .

Even though we're drivin' pretty fasht . . . I know this road like the back of my handsh . . . I reach down and pump the volume up hard on the shtereo, hit it harrrrdddd!!!!!!! . . . Really LOUD . . . Dr. Dre'sh . . . heavy bass . . . the whole Honda vibratin' like hellll . . . We're goin' down a shtraight shtretch . . . I lift my handsh off the shteering wheel and close my eyesh and we jus' fly along . . . no tears now, nothing but the tune, the night, the buzzzzz . . . We're flyin' along, eyesh closed . . . fashter . . . I'm that Leonardo *Titantic* guy . . . that "king of the world" guy. . . . I'm . . . invinshible . . . I mean i n v i n c i b l e . . .

Tim's never leavin' here . . . and I'm never leavin' eith-er . . . but right now I'm flyin' . . . I'm invincible AND invishible . . . I mean i n v i s i b l e . . .

We're never leavin' our livesh, we're never doin' nothin' but flyin' down the road till we die . . .

CHAPTER FIFTEEN

If the cops had busted us for drinking and driving last night, we'd be totally screwed, and we'd deserve to be. Even if Coach had caught us, we'd be suspended for at least a game and probably longer. So, of course, Coach didn't catch us. He doesn't want to catch us and we don't want to get caught. It's a great arrangement for everybody, even if it is totally stupid.

If we win our next game, this coming Friday, we'll lock up a trip to the state 4A basketball tournament being played this year in Spokane, three hundred miles away from here. Coach definitely wants Tim and me on the court for this next game and the tourney. It's a pretty big incentive for Coach to make sure he doesn't catch us howling at the moon.

But last night's drunk was a major bad-ass event. I mean Tim and I got *massively* wasted. I'm not sure why we needed to hit it so hard, but we did it and somehow we survived. I remember driving with my eyes closed, not even steering. It reminded me of that day at shoot-around when I couldn't miss anything. Amazing. Of course, we were lucky, stupidly lucky! I risked our lives and got away with it— and I don't even know why I did it.

Sometimes, and I know this sounds idiotic, but sometimes it's like there's this spirit riding along watching out for me. I never see or hear anyone, like if I were telling some stupid ghost story, but some part of me sometimes just . . . I don't know, *feels* something or someone near me. I know I sound crazy. I'm not crazy, but sometimes I sure act like it.

Right now, Shawn sits in his wheelchair, where he always sits, unless he's in his high chair being fed, or his bed sleeping. I look at him and wonder, for about the billionth time, what he's even here for. Sometimes everything just seems like such bull. I'm sure about only a few things in life, and these are that my dad's a jerk, my brother's a veg, and there is no God up in the sky watching over us. We're all just here for a while, alive for a few years, and then we're gone. That's it. Period. Nothing else makes any sense to me. Shawn's life has no meaning, but then maybe nobody's does. You're born, you live, and you die. That's it. There's no heaven, no hell, no nothing. That's what I believe, so I guess you might as well make the most of the time you're here. Well, I'm trying to, and the state championship tournament is my way out of this mess.

The thing about the tournament is that there are always scouts there from the big colleges. These scouts don't go to regular season games very often, but they go to tournaments because of all the good players there. I've already got acceptance letters from half a dozen colleges, but I've got my heart set on Georgetown. Of course, it's three thousand miles away, so I know I can't leave my family and go, but it'd be great to get an offer just the same. I mean, even to be told I'm good enough to get a free ride would be pretty cool.

And if by some miracle I *am* able to go away to college, I'd do it only if I could pay my own way, like through a scholarship. I won't take a dime from my old man. He's not gonna buy his way out of the guilt he should feel for leaving us by paying for my college. He's not getting off that easy. One thing, though, keeps racing through my mind, over and over again. When I was yelling at Dad and I said the thing about going away to college, he said, "That's what you *should* do." I can't believe he meant that, about my leaving. He has to know that with him gone, I'm left without any options. He has to know that I can't just leave like he did. I mean, how could I? He knows I'm not like him, so what he said was just crap, made him sound good, when he knows it's never going to happen.

Still, my only hope of escape, my only chance of ever getting away, comes down to one thing and one thing only: how good I can be on the basketball court.

CHAPTER SIXTEEN

We play Kennedy tonight. We're all sitting in the locker room waiting for Coach to give us his big pep talk, like we need help getting ready to play. If we win tonight, we've got an automatic bid to the state tournament. If you can't get up for this game, you have no pulse.

I should be tense, should have some kind of adrenaline edge by now, but I feel completely calm and relaxed. In last week's game I led all scorers and we killed Butler High School They aren't that strong a team, but we beat them by more than thirty points and they're not *that* bad.

I've been playing really loose for several weeks now, playing like I'm in some kind of trance. Ever since that day at shoot-around, when I couldn't miss and almost lifted off the ground, I've been "on." I've had great practices, and I haven't had a single bad game.

An hour or so from now, once we've won this game, I'll be the best player on the best team in our league. I'm not thinking about my dad, or my brother, or anybody or anything except winning. I'm calm and focused and ready.

I walk into the kitchen and Cindy and Mom are sitting there waiting for me. They're all smiles.

"Congratulations, honey," Mom says, and gives me a hug.

The phone rings, and I'm bugged at anybody for calling right now, interrupting this moment. So I grab it.

It's one of Cindy's friends, Ally Williamson. She asks for Cindy. She doesn't even congratulate me on our game.

I tell her, "Cindy—oh, didn't you hear?"

Cindy tries to grab the phone and yells, "MOM!"

I say, "She was in an accident today—a road-rage thing with a heavyweight boxer. Sorry." I hang up.

Mom, laughing, yells, "PAUL!"

I say, "It was a telemarketer."

They both buy it, so we all sit quiet for a second until I break the silence. "Well, we're going to state."

We beat Kennedy High School, our archrival, by six points. I led all scorers with twenty-four and missed a triple double by only two rebounds (fourteen assists and eight boards).

I repeat, "Did you hear me, we're going to state!"

Mom says, "I know, I know." She smiles and pauses a second, then says, "And guess what? We ladies are going to be there, en masse, to support you guys."

I'm confused. I ask, "Ladies?"

Mom says, "Your sister and I and some of Cindy's girl friends."

"You're coming to the tournament?"

Cindy says, "We're comin'."

I ask, "What about Shawn?"

Like I said before, the tournament is way over on the other side of the state this year.

Mom answers, "Respite care has already arranged for Shawn. Vonda will come and take care of him. We're coming to your game, Paul—get used to it."

I can't stop from asking, "Vonda? You're kidding me, right?"

Vonda has taken care of Shawn before. She's this enormous, bizarre woman, thighs the size of utility poles and a hairdo that reminds you of the Bride of Frankenstein. I don't like the idea of anybody taking care of Shawn but Mom or Cindy or me. What if he gets really bad? What if—

Mom interrupts my thoughts. "Shawn will be fine. Vonda will stay all weekend if necessary—"

"Oh, you can count on that. It'll definitely be 'necessary.' Once we make it to the final game—"

Cindy interrupts. "Overconfidence?"

I look at her and say, very matter-of-fact, "I get why you'd want to be there—you want to see the greatest butt-kicking high school dream team of all time—"

Cindy, laughing, interrupts. "Oh God, here he goes—"

The phone rings, and Cindy grabs it before I can.

"Hi, Ally," she says.

I start moving toward the stairs. I hear Cindy in the background say, "An accident? NO! MOM!"

I laugh.

Mom, looking at me, says, "Keep it up and I'll send you over to your father's."

I stare at Mom. I can't believe she'd say something like that tonight. I can't believe that on such a great night, she'd remind me of him. I say, "Now you're thinking, Mom."

She looks guilty. Maybe she feels bad for saying such a dumb-ass thing. But I'm not into rescuing her. I say, "I'm outa here."

I take off up the stairs.

Nothing is going to ruin this night for me. We're playing in the tournament. Nothing can take that away, not even worrying about leaving my brother or being reminded that the famous butt munch Sydney McDaniel is my old man.

CHAPTER SEVENTEEN

In the bottom drawer of my chest of drawers, hidden under a bunch of old T-shirts and socks, are letters from six universities and colleges. Every place I've applied I've got at least the possibility of a scholarship, but no word from Georgetown. They've had more time than anyone else, but still no word. They haven't said no, but they haven't said yes either—they haven't said anything!

It's not exactly late, yet, to be hearing back from colleges. Most places don't think about high school recruits until the season finishes up. But I'm still nervous.

I glance at some of the letters I've gotten from

other schools. I take out the one from Gonzaga, over in Spokane where the tourney is being played. This one came just a couple days ago.

```
Dear Paul McDaniel,
As Assistant Athletic Director for the
Gonzaga University Bulldogs Athletic
Department, I'd like to thank you for your
interest in our university's programs,
specifically our basketball program. . . .
```

Blah, blah,blah.

```
. . . an outstanding education . . .
your transcripts from high school appear
excellent . . . a unique learning
environment . . .
```

Blah, blah, blah.

```
. . . we would like to meet with you about
Gonzaga University as the right place to
pursue both your academic and athletic
goals . . .
```

Blah, blah, blah.
Actually, Gonzaga is my second pick, right after Georgetown.

I shove the letters back into my drawer, cover them with clothes, and grab my basketball to go out and shoot for a little while.

When I hit the bottom of the stairs, I turn the corner and notice Shawn sitting in his wheelchair by the window. He's quiet now, not "ahhhhing" or anything, just sitting there. I walk over to him. It's almost like he's watching the view. The sky is mostly blue with some puffy clouds. Puget Sound is dark blue in some places, where the clouds block the sun, and real sparkly in other spots, where the sun has broken through the clouds and shines on the water. It's like the dark places are depressing to look at, cold and black, but the sunny spots look like diamonds.

I look back down at Shawn. His eyes are open. His lips are a little apart and his chest rises and falls slowly with his breathing.

I wonder if he's getting any of this view action. I wonder if he sees the water and if he thinks about the different ways the water looks with the sun or without the sun. I wonder if he notices the difference in how his own skin feels when the sun shines on him or when it goes behind the clouds.

It's stupid of me to think he does. It's funny though—I've heard Mom say that Shawn's brain on fancy, high-tech machines like CAT scans and MRIs looks normal. I mean, there's no reason that you can see, on any of the medical tests, why Shawn should be so retarded. Of course, probably these tests don't show very much about the inside workings of the brain—Shawn's gray matter is probably all screwed up. It has to be, otherwise there's no way he'd be so out of it.

I look closely into his eyes. There's a kind of glassy expression there. You never get the feeling that he's looking back at you, even when you put your face in front of his, a couple inches away, like I'm doing right now.

"Hey, Shawn," I say.

Nothing.

"How you doin', buddy?"

Nothing.

"Can you see me?"

Nothing.

I stand next to Shawn for a while, looking out at the clouds and the water. Before long I notice that his breathing has changed and I look down at him; he's sound asleep.

I gently run my hand over his hair the way Mom always does. It feels so soft.

"Paul," I hear Mom whisper softly from behind me. I jerk my hand away from Shawn; it's almost like I'm embarrassed that she's caught me being nice to him.

I turn and face her.

She says gently, "It's okay to love your brother."

I don't know what to say.

She hesitates a second. "It's also okay to hate the way he is; sometimes I hate it too."

"I don't hate *him*," I answer quickly, feeling my face turn red.

"Of course you don't, honey," Mom says, her voice steady. "I know you don't hate Shawn, but it's okay to hate how he is sometimes."

Mom's wearing her jogging gear, and she looks about ten years younger than she really is. How can she be so good to Shawn? How can she be so good to all of us? My mom's the most amazing person I know. It's like the only rule she's ever had for me is to pretend that everything's fine with Shawn. And now she's saying it's not a rule anymore.

"I . . ." I hesitate. "I hate that I don't have a brother who knows he's my brother. I hate that

Shawn doesn't know I exist because he can't know anything. Most of all I hate how bad I feel not to love him more."

For a second I'm worried that what I've said will hurt Mom's feelings.

But she quickly says, "I hate those feelings too, darling. I feel the same things."

I'm shocked. "You?"

Mom says quietly, "I'm not immune to feeling sad, Paul. I feel heartbroken about your brother sometimes too. I do the best I can, but it's hard. I feel it, Paul, and so does your father."

My ears burn when she brings up Dad. "Come on! He left us!" I say. "He just ran away and—"

"No," Mom interrupts. "I sent him away, Paul. I made him leave."

No one has ever said this before. I always just assumed that Dad ran out on us. I don't know what to say. I stare at her. Finally I mutter, "You told him to leave because he didn't care, right? Because he hated Shawn and he didn't care about him?"

Mom walks over to me. She puts her arm around my shoulders. "You're so strong," she says softly. "So strong and brave and you try so hard."

It feels good for Mom to hug me. She says I'm

strong, but she's a thousand times stronger than me.

She says, "Your dad left when I told him to go. He couldn't help me care for Shawn the way I needed help. That was my fault as much as his. I needed to take care of Shawn in my own way. Your dad needed me too, but I couldn't give him what he needed; I couldn't take care of Shawn and your father at the same time."

I say, "You're just making excuses for him. You're just letting him run away from what he was supposed to do."

Mom pauses. I look at her face and see an expression I've never seen before—a kind of sadness, but not *just* sadness; there's something else there too—a look of acceptance. She stares into my eyes.

"Your dad didn't abandon us. He's done everything he can do to support us—"

I try to interrupt. "But he left!"

Mom says, "Yes, he left, Paul, because I sent him away. He didn't have the strength to help with Shawn. Your dad couldn't handle the heartbreak— every time he looked at your brother, he wept. He couldn't get over it. And now, Paul, you need to face what you have to do."

"What do you mean?"

Mom pulls me closer to her and kisses my cheek. "You have to lead your life for yourself. Don't let your brother's condition stop you from going after your dreams—otherwise you won't be able to love him. What your brother needs from you, what all of us need from you, is to be everything you can in life—college, athletics, wherever your dreams lead you, you have to go!"

I ask, "But how will you manage without me? I'm the only guy left around here."

Mom smiles and hugs me again. "I'll manage."

Suddenly Shawn shifts in his wheelchair. Both Mom and I, by instinct and habit, pause and look at him to make sure he's all right. He moves again and this time makes a little moaning sound, like he's dreaming. He's still asleep. When I look at Mom, we both smile at how well he has us trained.

Mom says, "I need you to be strong and happy, to have the fullest life you can have, just like I needed that from your dad. I want you to be okay, I need you all to be okay, so that I can focus on taking care of Shawn—because he needs me the most. But I love you and I want you to be happy and live your own life. Do you understand?"

Of course I understand; she's saying the thing

I've wanted somebody to say to me my whole life. Tears come to my eyes, and my throat tightens. Instead of answering, all I can do is nod.

"Good," Mom says. She pauses a moment. "Oh yeah, and one more thing."

I clear my throat and manage to mutter, "What?"

Mom smiles, "For your own peace of mind, and to help you handle some of your anger, you need to make peace with your dad. You think it was easy for him to leave. It wasn't. And it won't be for you either. You need to talk to him."

CHAPTER EIGHTEEN

Tim Gunther won't be playing with us for a while. Tim-bo's not going to be doing anything. He's in jail.

I haven't talked to him yet, but he called Cindy from jail and told her what happened. Cindy told me.

Tim came home from school yesterday to find his stepdad pissed off as usual, drunk as usual, and sitting on the living room couch like the giant human turd he is, as usual—no big news flashes there. The thing was, though, Tim couldn't find his mom. He called for her, and when she didn't answer, he walked all around through the house, getting more and more worried until he came to the bathroom door, which was locked. Tim yelled for her and his mom finally answered in a real scared-sounding voice.

She wouldn't open the door for a long time. And Tim's stepdad was in the background yelling at Tim, "Just leave the bitch alone."

Finally Tim got her to open the door and come out. She had two black eyes and the front of her blouse was all bloody and she'd been crying. Tim's stepdad had punched her when she'd refused to give him the keys to his truck.

Tim went back into the living room and beat the crap out of his stepdad.

Cindy wasn't sure whether Tim used any kind of weapon, but when it was over, Tim was standing and his stepdad wasn't. Some kids are already saying that Tim's stepdad has a fractured skull. Of course, some kids also claim that the guy has twenty-three broken ribs, a pretty amazing feat considering that humans have only twenty! Whatever the truth is, the guy was hauled away in an ambulance and Tim in a cop car.

As Cindy told me this, she cried a lot. I didn't know what to say to her, so I didn't say much at all. I know she and Tim care about each other, but since neither of them talks to me about that, what could

I say? I patted her on the back and told her every-thing would be okay, which, of course, is probably bull; I have no idea *how* everything is going to be.

The whole thing is pretty weird. It's weird that Tim would finally unload on his butt-streak residue of a stepdad. Although everybody has limits, Tim's about as mellow as anybody I know. It's also weird how on that night Tim and I got drunk, Tim said he wasn't ever getting out of here. If he can't play in the tournament, in front of college recruiters, his chances of getting a scholarship are almost nil. So maybe he was right. Maybe I was right too; maybe neither of us is getting out. But of all the guys I know, Tim would be the last one I'd ever imagine being stuck here for something like this. I'd be the first.

CHAPTER NINETEEN

We're done with practices for the rest of the week. No more shoot-arounds, no more scrimmages against one another. It's down to the wire now. This coming week is the trip to Spokane and the tournament. Losing Tim is bad, but the team has done a good job not getting distracted, and everyone knows that losing him means we've got to ratchet our games up a notch. Nobody says something else that we all know too: that without Tim, I'm going to have to be the best I've ever been.

No Shoreline High School team has ever won state before. The best anybody ever did was make the semifinals, and that was like a thousand years ago. So the pressure is on. Even I feel it. Before our last game with Kennedy I had a weird kind of calmness, but now, with the tourney approaching, I feel like I'm being stuck with a hundred little needles every time I think about it.

I'm out in front of the house shooting some practice shots by myself. Nothing wants to go in. I'm shooting simple little ten-footers and six-footers and even layins. Every shot I put up rims out.

And who should drive up before I can figure out what I'm doing wrong with my shot? My dad, of course.

I haven't seen him or spoken to him since the day we had the argument in the driveway. Even though Mom told me to talk to him, I still don't want to, and why does it have to be right now? Whatever Mom said about sending him away, Dad still bailed on us; nothing he can say to me will change that.

I try to ignore him and just keep shooting the ball, but out of the corner of my eye I see him park his car, get out, and start walking toward me. Damn.

"Pauly," he calls out.

I ignore him.

"Pauly—" he says again, and realizing I can't

escape, I take the ball and set it on the ground. I look at him.

"I—" he starts, but I interrupt.

"Nobody calls me that."

"What?"

I say, "You heard me. Nobody calls me that. It's Paul, not Pauly."

Dad takes a deep breath, like a sigh, and says, "But I've always called you Pauly."

"Right," I say, and just stare at him.

He takes another breath and says, "Okay, Paul. Paul, can I talk to you for a minute?"

I answer, "No . . . definitely not, no."

Dad says, "Come on, Paul. I promise, it'll just take a minute, okay?"

I think, Shit, shit, shit, but I hear myself say, "Whatever . . ."

As Dad walks over and sits on the porch steps, he turns off his cell phone. He *never* turns it off, so this talk must mean something to him. He waits for me to come sit down. I don't want to, I really don't, but somehow my feet carry me to the porch.

Dad says, "Listen, I'm sorry about being such an asshole the other day."

I think, The other day? What about *every day*?!

It's like he's reading my mind. "I'm sorry for all the times I've acted shitty. I'm a human being, Paul, and sometimes not a very good one."

I don't know what to say—he's *never* apologized to me before. I sit quiet. I wish he'd just leave.

"Paul," Dad says gently, his voice almost a whisper, "I know this is hard for you, sitting here with me. I'm asking you to just give me a couple minutes to try and explain—"

I don't know what he's talking about. I ask, "Explain what?"

Dad pauses a second and looks me in the eye. "I never abandoned you or your brother. I know that to you my leaving felt like abandonment, but the truth is I think about you guys every day, *every day*—trying to figure out how to help, how best to take care of Shawn and all of you."

I feel my face get red, not really anger as much as some weird kind of confusion. "You still left, Dad. You still walked out. You may think about us but you're not *here*."

Dad looks me in the eye. "I know, Paul. I'm sorry. I mean that—I'm truly sorry. I was a mess before your mother sent me away. I'm better now, but back then, I was just so tired all the time—"

I interrupt. "Mom sent you away, but did that mean you had to go?"

Dad says, "I'm not blaming her, Paul. She's great. But she and I talked a lot after we realized how bad Shawn's problems were, and your mom knew even before I did that we couldn't handle it in the same ways. This isn't an excuse, Paul—I left because of my cowardice and my weakness. But your mom knew that I needed to go, that she couldn't take care of both Shawn and me."

Dad pauses a second, then says, "Paul, I haven't abandoned this family. I haven't abandoned your brother, believe me; I love him every bit as much as I love you and your sister. I'm constantly thinking about what I can do, what I should do, what I might have to do to take care of him. But whatever I do with Shawn, he's *not* your responsibility."

I think, Of course you'd say that! But I remember that Mom said this too. I feel a rush of emotion, a weird mix of sadness and happiness. I don't know what to say, but somehow, listening to Dad's words, I feel a huge weight lift off me. Dad is speaking straight into my heart, and his words take away a terrible pressure.

Dad puts his arm around me and pulls me close

to him. I haven't touched him or been touched by him in too many years to remember, not since I was little and he used to lift me up and swing me around and carry me upstairs to bed and tuck me in and kiss me good night and say, "See you in the morning, Pauly—I love you." And in his arms again now, I close my eyes and all those little-kid feelings of safety wash back over me again.

We sit quietly for a while.

Finally I look at Dad and say, "I don't know what to do, Dad. . . .What should I do?"

Dad answers right away. "For yourself, start making plans for college." He pauses a second. "For me? Well, you know what I want. You know what I always want."

Yeah, I know, and I have to admit, it actually feels okay to hug him back. Even though it's been a long time, it still feels familiar.

Dad says, "Whatever you decide to do, Paul, I'll support you one hundred percent. You're old enough to know what's best for yourself. But remember, whatever happens, Shawn is your mother's and *my* responsibility, not yours. All you have to do is try to love him as best you can."

I can't forgive my dad; it's too confusing. It's too

much to think about, too much to feel. All these years I've been mad at Dad, but mostly I realize that I've been mad at myself, mad and ashamed at how I felt about my brother. My dad just did what I've wished I could do a thousand times—he ran away from Shawn. I can't forgive my dad, but I understand him better. It's me I don't understand; how I can love my brother so much one minute and then, the next minute . . .

Suddenly I feel a rush of fear and a sick sensation in my gut. I look at Dad as we sit quietly, but inside I feel scared and shaky; there's one thing left that needs to be done, one terrible secret that *I* need to talk about—not with my dad, but with my brother.

Dad has gone and I'm alone now with Shawn in his regular spot by the window. Mom's upstairs and can't hear me. Cindy's not home from school yet.

I say, "Hey, bro, listen, I have to tell you something. . . ." The words just come out. I feel scared for a second, but I shake the fear away—it's now or never—I have to do this.

Without planning how I'm going to start, I just begin. "That time, Shawn, when those two bullies were picking on you, the Bic lighter, them hurting you; what you couldn't see that day, what no one saw, was . . ."

I hesitate. I don't know if Shawn understands me or not, but I need to tell him this anyway, I need to tell him the truth, the part I never imagined I'd tell anyone. . . .

"There's something more," I say, staring into Shawn's eyes.

My throat is tight. "I . . . I . . ." I stutter and start to lose my nerve.

Shawn suddenly makes his "ahhhhhhh" sound, like he's trying to answer me. Like he's trying to say, "It's okay, bro, just let it out. . . ."

I stare into his eyes, take one more deep breath, and finally speak. "I saw what they were doing, Shawn, and I wanted them to do it."

Shawn stares off into space.

For the first time ever, hopefully for the *last* time ever, I say these horrible words that I've been too afraid to ever say, even to myself. "I saw those two guys before they even came into the yard that day. I heard them teasing you and I knew they were going to mess with you. I saw them walk up and I wasn't afraid of them, but I just stood at the corner of the house watching. I saw that one kid get out the cigarette lighter and put it under your chin. And I just stood there. I thought it could be over at last— I wouldn't be the guy with the broken brother. . . ."

I pause a second and try to catch a breath. My hands are shaking and my stomach feels terrible. I'm afraid to look into Shawn's eyes, so I stare at the floor. "When he held that lighter under your chin, and you started moving all around, trying to escape, I said inside my head, 'Go ahead and do it! Just kill him and let this all be over.' I wanted them to kill you, Shawn. I wanted you . . . gone!"

I burst into sobs and can't say more. But there's nothing more to say. My brother, if he knows anything, if he understands words at all, knows the truth about me now; that I'm nothing, less than nothing, a coward and a selfish jerk, too afraid to even love him.

Tears stream down my cheeks. I feel dizzy and sick. I bury my face in my hands and try to breathe. I collapse onto the floor next to Shawn's wheelchair and just sit there, crying.

Through my sobs I manage to spit out, "I'm so ashamed. . . ."

I'm crying too hard to say more; I can hardly breathe.

I cry for a long, long time, sitting there on the floor, alone with my brother.

I finally stop crying. I begin to breathe evenly again. My ribs and chest ache from all my sobbing, but a strange kind of peacefulness starts to fill me.

Finally I say, "I'm sorry, Shawn. I am. I'll never let anyone hurt you, bro, and *I'll* never pretend again that I don't know you. You're my brother, Shawn, and I'm yours. That's the way it is."

We sit silently. Something has changed in me. I don't know how to describe it, but something has happened between us. I watch Shawn sitting in his wheelchair, staring out at the world—does he understand anything about what I just told him? Does he get how much I care about him? Maybe not.

But at least *I* finally get it.

CHAPTER TWENTY

It's Thursday afternoon and I'm wearing my travel clothes for the trip to Spokane: slacks, blazer, shirt, and a stupid baby-blue tie. In the last few days everything has changed; everything I thought before, everything I've worried about for years, feels different. Plus there's a million new thoughts slamming through my brain.

For instance, I keep wondering, What if it's partly, maybe mainly, *because* of Shawn that I am who I am? What if God couldn't help Shawn be normal, so the next best thing he could do was give me everything, all of Shawn's talents and all of my own too?

I walk over to where Shawn is sitting and I look

down at him. He's drooling pretty heavily and there's a giant wet spot on the front of his coveralls and T-shirt. We're alone.

I pat his head softly. I kiss his forehead and feel this huge love for him. I tell him what I've never been able to say since that day the bullies were hurting him. "I love you, bro."

Shawn says "ahhhhhh" back at me, almost like he understands, almost like he's answering.

I smile and kiss his forehead again and say, "See you in a few days." I'm going to miss him; it's weird, but I really am.

CHAPTER TWENTY-ONE

There's one last thing I need to do before I catch the bus for the tournament. Cindy rides with me to pick up Tim from the courthouse.

Tim has to go to his mom's, where he'll have to stay until his court date. His stepdad is getting better, but he's still in the hospital. Earlier, when Tim called for a ride, he told Cindy that he's being charged with second-degree assault, a felony. His lawyer says they'll get it knocked down to a misdemeanor, but that it's going to take some time. So Tim can't leave King County; hell, he can't even leave his house! Even though he's out of jail, there's no tournament for him.

I spot him walking down the sidewalk and across the parking strip. He looks worried. But when he sees us waiting, he smiles.

Cindy jumps out of the car and runs to greet him, giving him a hug. He looks at me, over her shoulder, for a second or two, then closes his eyes and hugs her back. They just stand there holding each other. I look away, out the front of the car, trying to give them a little privacy. It feels good to me that they have each other.

They both start to climb into the backseat until Tim realizes what he's doing. He opens the door for Cindy, closes it, then he sits up front so I won't look like a chauffeur. Cindy, sitting right behind him, scoots up close so that she can hold his hand. We take off.

"You okay?" I ask.

"I guess," Tim answers.

"Any place special you wanna go?"

"Yeah," Tim says. "*Not* back there." He nods his head in the direction of the jail. He was in three nights and four days.

I pause a second, trying to think what to say next. Finally I ask, "Do you feel that you benefited

128

all you could from the institution?"

Tim smiles, recognizing this from *Raising Arizona*, one of our favorite videos. He answers, "I released myself on my own recognizance." He pauses a moment, then jumps to a different scene from that movie—"Life is strange, huh? They oughtta sell tickets."

I take my cue. "I'd buy a couple."

We both laugh.

But something feels different; something feels unsaid. For all the times I fought and hurt people, if anybody deserved to go to jail, it's me. This hangs over us and weighs on me.

I say, "This shouldn't have happened to you, Tim-bo. I'm sorry."

My apology doesn't make any sense, and Tim knows it doesn't. He quickly says, "It's not your fault, Paul. It's my mistake, period."

"I don't know, man," I say. "If anybody deserves . . ." I hesitate. "I mean, with all the fighting I've done, you know, I could have killed somebody."

Tim smiles and says, "You didn't, though."

I say, "Neither did you."

Tim looks out the window and I notice him

squeezing Cindy's hand. "Nope, I didn't. But I sure wanted to."

We ride along in silence for a few blocks; then I look over at Tim again and notice that he's looking back at Cindy. His words echo in my mind, as I think about all the times I wanted to kill the whole world.

I don't feel that way anymore. A chill runs down my spine at how close I came to messing up my whole life. If somebody was looking out for me, they did a good job. But now it's up to me.

The ride to Spokane on the chartered bus is long. There's not a lot to do on bus rides like this. Some of the guys talk together, some sleep, half are wearing headphones, chilling to tunes.

John-Boy Reich is sitting next to me, on the seat where Tim-bo should be.

Neither of us says much as the bus cruises down I-90, past empty brown fields with little blue signs on the fence lines: ALFALFA, CORN, POTATOES.

I glance around the bus, looking at all my teammates. The Hankster is snoring about as loud as you'd expect. Wille Anderson and Carl Restov are playing cards, hearts I think. I look at all these guys: Johnny, Jesse, Antwon, George, Lewis, Brian, Terrel, Matt, Philip, all of them. Right now, after I've seen Tim, they *all* feel like family to me; each and every one of them is like a brother as we're going into battle this one last time together.

I look back over at John-Boy and he's staring out the window. I wonder if he's thinking what I'm thinking as he sits in Tim-bo's seat: that I'm so incredibly lucky to be here, what a miracle it is that I'm not going through what's happening to Tim Gunther.

I hope Tim'll be okay. He's always been the brother to me that Shawn couldn't be, the one I could do stuff with, but somehow, now, all my teammates are my brothers too. I wish Tim were here with us—he deserves to be. Then again, maybe "deserves" doesn't have much to do with it. Maybe in life you get what you get, and you just have to learn to deal with it.

After almost three hundred miles and five hours, we finally reach a stand of scrubby pine trees, a couple tiny "lakes," and then, half an hour later, we start down a steep hill into Spokane.

We're staying at the Davenport Hotel. It's really a beautiful place, but I'm not sure any of us has even noticed. My bros and I have got some unfinished business to take care of.

CHAPTER TWENTY-TWO

Tonight's game, the final for the state championship, will be my last in any sport as a high school player. I'm graduating in April, so no baseball this year. My high school jock career has all come down to this night.

We're in our locker room at the Spokane Arena. The building is fairly new and seats fourteen thousand plus. For our earlier games, the qualifying rounds to see who would play in tonight's final, the floor of the arena was divided into two courts by a huge fabric screen, so that two games were played at the same time. Tonight the screen is gone. This last game, for the state championship, is the only one in town.

Our opponent is an old foe—Kennedy High School. As runner-up to the Seattle league title, they were top-seeded in the Blue bracket, which they won. We won the Red bracket.

The crowd is huge, a sellout. Earlier we got to peek out and watch them pour into the building. Now, as we sit in this locker room on shiny wooden benches, the crowd sounds like a big animal pawing right above our heads.

Coach gathers us around to make his final speech. We sit quietly; there's a lot of intensity in this small corner of the concrete room.

Coach says, "Do you all remember that day when Paul McDaniel couldn't miss during shoot-around?"

Everybody glances at me and I feel myself blush.

"Well, gentlemen, tonight shares with that moment one thing and one thing only. . . ."

Coach pauses for a second until he's sure that we're all looking at him—his face is a little bit red and his forehead is sweating.

"In basketball, in all sports, the best part is the possibility that something miraculous might happen. The possibility of a miracle is always right at your fingertips if you have the courage to feel it.

"That day when Paul was throwing up shots

and made that last one, even though I think he peeked"—Coach glances over at me and winks—"that day we glimpsed the miraculous on a small, individual scale. Today the miracle could be here again, only this time it really means something; this time it counts."

Coach pauses and takes a deep breath. "You guys have one job to do, one last job—go out and believe in the miraculous—believe in yourselves and one another. Think, play together, but most of all feel the possibility of the miracle. I promise that if you do that, when this game is over, you'll understand what I'm talking about. Do any of you have anything you'd like to say?"

Everybody is quiet for a few seconds. Maybe everyone is thinking about this being our last game, maybe they're worried that they might screw up in front of fourteen thousand screaming fans, maybe they're not thinking at all.

Finally John-Boy Reich says, "I'd like to dedicate this game to Tim Gunther." He glances over at me and gives a little smile.

Dedicating our game is something some of the guys always do. But tonight we're doing it for the last time ever, so it means something special. I think about all the times Tim and I played hoops in my driveway, about the million videos we've watched, about that day he held Cindy while Shawn was seizing. And now I think about Shawn, too, back home with Vonda. He's probably in bed already: Sleeping? Dreaming?

John-Boy interrupts my thoughts, shouting, "For Tim-bo!"

And like we always do, we all yell out together, "For Tim-bo!"

A couple other guys say some things that I only half register. Words are forming inside me and I want to say them just right.

Finally I speak up. "I'm playing tonight for my family, but most of all, more than anybody, for my brother, Shawn."

Everybody looks at me and nobody says anything. I've never dedicated a game to Shawn before. Some of the guys probably didn't even know I *had* a brother. But I yell, "For Shawn-bo!"

Everybody shouts out together, loud and strong, "For Shawn-bo!!"

Goose bumps cover my arms as we all stand up. We're ready!

CHAPTER TWENTY-THREE

Kennedy is playing unconscious. Their play-making is gorgeous, their execution perfect. At the end of the first half they lead us by twenty-two points. I'm having a good game, not great, but good. I'm scoring well, eight for eleven from the floor, three for four from the foul line. I have half a dozen assists, but I'd have a dozen more if the rest of the guys were shooting basketballs rather than throwing up bricks. By all reasoning this game is over. A twenty-two-point deficit is pretty much insurmountable. Pretty much . . . still . . .

The second half starts with an ugly little 6–0 run by Kennedy, boosting their lead to twenty-eight and a time-out by our coach. The Kennedy fans are going nuts—screaming and stomping and out of control, as we straggle over to the bench, hanging our heads.

We gather around and Coach says in a calm, quiet voice, "Okay, gentlemen, I think we've got them right where we want 'em." Everybody smiles. Then Coach says, "It's miracle time." He turns to me and says, "You ready, captain?"

I'm not sure what he means, but I answer, "Always."

Coach says, "Okay, guys, here's the plan—Paul isn't going to miss any more shots. It's miracle shoot-around time again, so set your screens, then get out of his way. Hankster, don't even worry about offensive boards—there are no rebounds when every shot drops. You just step out and clog the lanes, help Paul get some shooting space, okay?"

Huge drops of sweat fall from Hankster's forehead when he nods. He looks over at me and I smile.

We break the huddle; we're down twenty-eight with just over fifteen minutes to play. As we start to walk away, Coach calls out once more, "Okay, guys, miracle time!" He says this to all of us, but he's looking straight at me.

• • •

My first three shots, all of them three-pointers, drop, hitting nothing but net. The kid guarding me is an inch taller than I am but not nearly as quick. Even though Kennedy misses their next three shots, and their lead drops to nineteen, my opponent still looks confident.

The next time I have the ball, still in the back-court, I start to talk to him. "You guys got this game in the bag, you know?" I dribble to my right, cross over, and move quickly to my left. "You might as well go pick up that trophy right now, you know?" I dribble behind my back and, just above the top of the key, I fake a move toward the basket, step back, and launch my jumper. As I release, I'm still talking. "I mean, come on, man, no team has ever *blown* a twenty-two-point halftime lead in a state final, and . . ."

The ball swishes through and I say, "Oops, another three-pointer. What's that, four in a row?"

As we head up court, he mumbles softly, so the ref won't hear him, "Up yours, ball hog!"

I smile.

We're working ferociously on defense, but the refs are letting us play, not calling fouls. Even though they're hitting a few baskets, you can feel Kennedy tightening up; you can see it in their hesitation to shoot, hear it in their heavy breathing; you can almost smell their fear.

With eight minutes left in the game, their lead is down to sixteen points, seventy-six to sixty. I've lost track of how many points I have—I don't even care. I've made all our second-half points except for three, a little five-foot bank shot from our forward Brian Hillsdale and one of two foul shots by John-Boy Reich.

As I'm dribbling the ball up court, I can see the frustration on the face of the kid defending me. I don't know his name, but he's good—just not good enough to stop me.

"You gettin' tired?" I ask him as I dribble the ball up court.

He snarls at me.

"I sure am scorin' a lot, aren't I . . . you ever heard of defense?"

When I say this, he rushes up and tries to crowd me, but when he does, it opens an easy lane to the hoop and I break for it before he can get any inside help. I hit an easy layin.

"Wow," I say as I start to move back past my defender. But suddenly, without warning, he spits straight into my face. It's a big wad of spit too, hitting my cheek, eye, and nose. I look around to see if any of the refs saw this, but none of them are looking our way. My defender gets this smirking grin and says real softly, "I hear you got a retard for a brother. A real basket case."

I lift my hand to my face and wipe away the spit. I don't say anything, but I feel my anger rising.

He says, "Is your brother here so he can see how chicken you are?"

When he says this, I realize that Mom and Cindy probably *did* see what just happened; they always tell me everything I do in a game, from every shot I hit to when I unconsciously adjust my jock during time-outs.

Kennedy gets the ball back and makes an easy bucket.

It's our ball again, and I start to bring it up court when the kid who spit in my face comes at me hard. Not even pretending to go for the ball, he crashes into me and throws an elbow into my face. I hear a popping sound as my nose and right cheek take the blow. I lose my balance and fall.

The ref blows his whistle, but before he can get over to us, the kid who just fouled me walks onto and into me, kneeing me in the side of the head. Another whistle. I look up and the kid, his fists clenched, is standing over me.

He whispers viciously, "Come on, chicken— maybe *you're* the retard I heard about?"

I put the back of my hand against my nose. Trying to breathe, I swallow a big mouthful of blood.

The ref reaches us and pushes the kid away from me, signaling an intentional, flagrant foul, which means that the kid is gone. Since he's thrown out anyway, now he really goes ballistic, screaming at me, "You chicken shit! Chicken—" But a couple of his teammates pull him away; they look back at me, smirking too, like I'm a coward.

The thing is, though, I don't even feel like fighting. I'm not scared, not really hurt; it's not that I'm worried about getting tossed—I just don't need to fight. I look at the kid once more and at his teammates who walk with him. I don't feel angry, or like going after them. He fouled me to get me out of the game. I don't want to leave, so I suppose I win. But even that doesn't matter right now. *My* winning doesn't mean anything—what matters is that there are four minutes thirty-two seconds left on the clock and we're down by twelve points.

During the official injury time-out, our trainer jams two huge wads of cotton into my nose to stop the bleeding.

Coach asks, "You okay?"

I smile, even though I'm a little dizzy and my nose feels sore. I answer, "Yeah, I'm fine."

After the time-out, I take my technical foul shot and then two more free throws. I make all of them. Kennedy's lead is just nine points.

I'm relaxed and totally calm. Even though Kennedy makes a few of their shots, I'm hitting shots too as we pick away.

With two minutes and twenty seconds left, we've cut their lead to only five points. They miss another shot and the Hankster grabs the board, tossing the ball out to me. I bring it down court, but they've hustled back on defense, so I have to slow things down. I pass the ball, move to a screen, expecting a pass back, but Wille has an open easy little eight-footer so he takes it. It rims out and they get the board.

They bring the ball back, and their shooting guard hits a clutch three-pointer. Their bench explodes, guys jumping around, hitting each other with towels, leaping into the air, celebrating; their lead is back to eight with under two minutes to go.

I bring the ball up court, and just as I cross the half-court line I see an open lane to the basket. I start to drive but pull up at the three-point line and take my jumper. It ticks the rim but goes through.

My head is in the game, but it's also outside myself. Although I'm totally present and in the moment, I "see," in some part of my mind, all kinds of stuff: Mom and Cindy up in the stands; Shawn back in Seattle; Tim-bo and Eddie Farr and even that little girl with her ugly dog—it's weird, I'm 100 percent here *and* 100 percent somewhere, *everywhere*, else. All my life I've used sports to run away, but I have nothing left to run away from. As I move back on defense, I realize this is the most fun I've ever had playing—in fact, this is the first time in my whole life that I've truly been *playing*. I feel that sensation of flying again, that feeling of almost floating.

After a miss by Kennedy, I grab the rebound, bring it back, and almost unconsciously throw up another three-pointer that hits nothing but net. Their lead is two with under a minute left to play. As soon as their guy gets the ball, we pressure full court and foul.

Their kid hits his first shot but misses the second. The Hankster grabs the board, passes out to me, and I bring the ball back up and hit another shot. My foot was on the line so it's only a two-pointer. They lead by one with thirty-one seconds left to play. We haven't led this game for a single second. It's their ball.

We full-court press again and I manage to get a steal. It's almost the identical move to that day when I poked the ball away from Tim and gouged his little finger, only I don't touch the kid from Kennedy.

I dribble the ball back to the top of our key and our guys spread the floor. I'm thinking about the game but I'm also thinking about Shawn—imagining him somehow knowing what's going on. The kid guarding me, who came in after the flagrant-foul guy was tossed, has quick hands, but he's shorter than I am and not as strong. I'm dribbling the ball, relaxed, waiting for the clock to go down. I glance at the shot clock; there are seven seconds left. I glance at the game clock; sixteen seconds—this means that after I make my shot, we'll have to hustle right back on D, because they'll have almost ten seconds to bring the ball in, get it down, and . . .

In a flash, the kid guarding me jabs the ball

free, catching a lot of my hand as he does. I listen for a whistle, but the refs don't call it. The kid hurries over and grabs the loose ball. Once he corrals it, he takes off toward his basket.

Everything slows down, almost stops, as I think about what's happening: the game, Georgetown, my dad, Shawn . . .

I turn and chase the kid who's stolen the ball. I've got a slight angle on him, and as he reaches his basket, trying for a layin that would clinch the game for them, I time my jump from behind perfectly and block his shot. Even though I don't touch him, he falls down over the end line, flopping for a call. The ball bounces toward the out-of-bounds line on the right side. There's no whistle. I manage to grab the ball an instant before it goes out, leaning over the line and barely getting my balance. The game clock reads three seconds. I dribble toward our end. The clock ticks down . . . two seconds . . . one second. I'm still way out, not even up to half court yet, but I have to shoot *now*.

There's no time to think about it. So I let it go, a high, arching shot. The buzzer sounds while the ball is still soaring through the air. Everything is clear; everything is right here, my whole world, everything wide open—

My release felt good, felt perfect, actually— nice rotation, good height—the buzzer stops, and there's total silence; fourteen thousand fans, every player and every coach, watch the flight of my desperation shot.

I don't feel desperate, though, I feel perfectly calm and happy; whatever happens will happen, whatever—

Swish.

It's funny, you know, how you see guys on ESPN hit the miracle shot, the buzzer beater, then fall to their knees or jump in the air or run around with their arms spread out and their mouths wide open looking for someone to hug. Moments like this don't come very often in sports or in life. And now it's happening to *me*. Maybe I'm not ready for it, or maybe I'm *too* ready—whatever the reason, I don't do any of those celebration things. I'm glad that the shot fell. I'm glad that we've won the game. Although it's fun, it doesn't matter in the same way that so many bigger things matter.

My teammates disagree, mobbing me at center court in a pileup that resembles twenty madmen trying to escape a madhouse.

At the bottom of this crazed, laughing, screaming, smelly, sweating pile of brothers, I think about everybody and everything: Mom, Cindy, Dad, Tim-bo, Seattle, and especially Shawn, my *real* brother—I think about all of us. And suddenly I realize that I've never been so happy. Ready or not, world, here I come!

It takes me longer than any of the other guys to finally make it into the locker room. Recruiters from Gonzaga *and* Georgetown are waiting for me in the hallway outside right now. I shook their hands and they both said they'd wait until after I showered. We couldn't talk out there anyway, in all that postgame chaos: cheerleaders, the band, my mom and sister, and about a thousand kids I don't even know slapping my back and looking crazed. I finally made it in here, where the guys and I celebrated.

Now everyone's gone except for me. I'm taking my time. I suppose I should feel a little guilty about making people wait for me, but I can't let go of this moment. All my life I've been in sports to escape something. Without even knowing it, I was always looking over my shoulder. Tonight, for the first time ever, I played for the excitement and rush of just playing. I guess it's like Coach said: This night is a miracle.

I remember that day at shoot-around when I felt like I could fly—and now I know I can!

In fact, right now, I'm already soaring—I feel so good.

Once I step out of this locker room, the rest of my life will begin—college, new friends, big decisions, everything will be different. Almost everything; there's one thing I can always count on that never changes. I think back to talking with Shawn the other day, telling him how I really felt about him.

I love my brother—finally I can say that and truly mean it; I really do love him.

Before anything else tonight, I'm going to phone our house back in Seattle and have Vonda wake Shawn up. I'm going to tell her to hold the phone next to his ear and I'm going tell my brother about everything that's happened. But most of all, I'll tell him how much I love him, whether he understands what I'm saying or not.

I'll tell him what it feels like to soar!

Cruise through these other mesmerizing titles by Terry Trueman

Pb 0-06-447213-2

Stuck in Neutral

In this Printz Honor novel, we meet Shawn McDaniel: a teenager with cerebral palsy, and an undiscovered miracle. No one who looks at Shawn has any idea of what he is truly like. And as long as Shawn is unable to communicate his feelings to his father, his life is at risk.

Inside Out

In a busy coffee shop, a robbery goes wrong. Two gunmen hold nine hostages, including Zach Wahhsted, a seemingly ordinary teenager. What nobody realizes is that Zach has a mind more dangerous than any weapon.

Hc 0-06-623962-1
Pb 0-06-447376-7

Hc 0-06-057491-7

No Right Turn

Three years after his father's suicide, Jordan is a self-described zombie. No real friends, no interests, nothing. But then salvation comes in the most unlikely form: a 1976 Corvette. Slowly, Jordan realizes that maybe, just maybe, he can start living again. But does he want to?